MINDSCAPE THREE

DEAD SQUARES
KING'S ENDGAME

OUTLANDERS OF THE MULTIVERSE
COLLECTION

BY D.N. LEO

Narrative Land Publishing
Narrativeland.com

PART ONE

DEAD SQUARES

CHAPTER 1

Jo spat the black liquid she'd thought was coffee back into the mug and put the mug back on the console of her control station. The dim light from the sky dome seeped through the semi-transparent ceiling and reflected on the polished floor and the shiny computer monitors on the wall. She normally preferred monitors to wallpaper, but at the moment, it seemed a little too much for her. She'd been staring at the monitors for so long that her eyes felt like they were bleeding.

She needed some caffeine to jolt her system. She had to catch up on her research for the job at hand—being Sciphil Four—a position that made her responsible for more than a hundred billion civilians in her district.

Jo considered herself a good computer designer. On Earth, as the Steel Princess, she was unbeatable in the hologame community. She had only ever lost to Ciaran, who played as White Knight. That was good enough for her when it came to computer games. She wasn't nearly as good as Ciaran in computer programming, but that was only because he had more resources than she did.

She clucked her tongue to herself. In the hologame and in matrixes, being able to see patterns was a crucial skill. She was definitely as good as he in recognizing patterns. Ciaran was good because he had a wealth of knowledge about...well, about almost everything. But he had the unfair advantage of being conceived in the Red Stage of the Daimon Gate. And from what Jo had heard, children conceived there were considered to be the best beings in the cosmos.

Her parents were bakers and lived in New York. They had a modest cake shop in town that had earned them enough money to put her through college. But her ability to see patterns hadn't come through education. It was her natural talent—or maybe her curse. Because of that so-called talent, she'd ended up here—in this strange universe where none of her life experiences or skills applied.

She missed her coffee and the bagels from her brother's bakery. For the life of her, she couldn't get her robot to make a decent cup of coffee. She missed hanging out with her best friend, Madeline, and watching silly chick flicks. And she missed the time she had been Tadgh-free.

"Ted!" she growled as she leaned down to her computer keyboard and banged her head against it a few times. Sometimes her robot's name sounded much too close to Tadgh.

"Yes, Jo!" Her home robot rolled in. He was as round as a soccer ball and stood at knee height. Although he had working limbs, he usually chose to roll instead of walking.

"I gave you the precise recipe for coffee, yet you brought me this disgusting black liquid! How hard can it be to make a cup of coffee? If you show me where the ingredients are, I'll make it myself. Is there a coffee shop in town? There has to be one."

"I make the coffee according to your formula. However, some of the organic ingredients you gave me aren't available in Eudaiz, so I took the liberty of using some substitutes."

"Well, that's the problem. Coffee isn't simply black liquid with caffeine. But taste is something I doubt you'll ever understand."

"I am afraid that human tastes and preferences are too complicated to program into a home robot like me."

"I'm sure Ciaran's Robert has the correct program!"

"Robert isn't just a home robot, he's the first generation of—"

"All right. I get it. No need to elaborate, Ted." Then she sighed. "I'm sorry. I'm a little testy—"

"Obviously!" Tadgh's voice interrupted. Without invitation, he sauntered in and began to massage Jo's shoulders.

"Why wasn't Tadgh's arrival announced?" Jo asked Ted.

"It was." Ted pointed to the door monitor. There she saw the blinking message that Tadgh had just arrived at her residence. She had been testing a program that would allow her friends in without scanning. Apparently, the system considered Tadgh to be her friend.

"So what are you testy about, Sciphil Four?" Tadgh asked. "Nothing I did, I hope."

She shook her head. "I can't put my finger on some programs."

"Anything I can help with?" Ted asked.

Jo arched an eyebrow. "What kind of analyses can you run?"

"I don't have the ability to conduct any analytical processes. But I do have access to data. I can gather the data for you using any data retrieval algorithm you wish. The speed of my—"

Jo raised her hand to stop the robot. "You're saying I can dictate search commands to you, and you'll pull the data for me? I don't have to deal with this monstrous search engine with its odd search terms and algorithms?" Jo's voice had increased noticeably in pitch, and she shifted in her chair to gather her composure. She removed

Tadgh's hands from her shoulders so that he stopped massaging them.

Tadgh pulled up a chair and sat down next to Jo. She cleared her throat and lowered her voice. "Now, Ciaran's coronation will be next week. I imagine it'll be a huge event in Eudaiz, and there will be many badasses in the cosmos lurking around to try to ruin the day. I'm assuming security will be strict, but I want to see if there's any potential danger the ordinary system might have missed."

"Affirmative," Ted said.

"Ciaran wouldn't want his coronation ruined, so I suppose Tower Three is already secured. But have the security risks of the other eight towers been assessed?"

"Yes. In order from the most to least secured— Tower One, Tower Seven, Tower Nine, Tower Two, Tower Six, Tower Five, Tower Eight and Tower Four."

Jo nodded then frowned at Tadgh's expression. "What's wrong?" she asked.

"You're the most unsecured Sciphil during the coronation," Tadgh said.

She frowned again and recalled Ted's report. Tadgh was right. The robot had said Tower Four was the least secure. "How can I rank even lower than Sciphil Eight, the guy we haven't even met?"

"Sciphil Eight has been on a mission and will return by coronation time. He has no record of a security breach in the last fifty years," Ted said.

"On what basis does security rank me as most risky?" Jo asked.

"The security committee has twelve members. The head of the committee, Sizx, Eudaiz's head of intelligence, has developed a..."

"Who? The blue-haired chick? Oh, come on! Give me a break!" Jo exclaimed and pushed up off her chair.

Tadgh pulled her into his arms. "Calm down, darling." Then he turned toward Ted. "What are the criteria for security ranking?"

"History of Sciphil succession. Origin of the current Sciphil. And security records," Ted answered.

"All right. What's the succession history of the Sciphil Four position?" Jo asked and sat down on Tadgh's lap.

"Hoyt Flanagan. Tor Linii. Manix Lunn. Bly Srico. Kyle Wolf. And you, Josephine Cassidy."

"Well, I know I'm human. Kyle Wolf is Eudaizian. How many other humans are in the successor line?"

"Hoyt Flanagan and you are both human. The rest were Eudaizian."

"Okay, so what's the succession line of, say, the Sciphil Three position?" Tadgh asked.

"Pierre LeBlanc. Aedan LeBlanc. Ealga LeBlanc. Malachi LeBlanc. Bran LeBlanc. And the current king-to-be, Ciaran LeBlanc."

Jo turned around and saw Tadgh looking at her. There was one thing that Tadgh and Jo had in common—they were both good at recognizing patterns. And Tadgh was brilliant at numbers. He could even calculate the probability of pattern occurrence in his head.

Now, they both saw a pattern emerging.

"Apart from Sciphil Three, are other Sciphil positions running within a family?" Jo asked.

"It has been the case in the past. But the latest generation of Sciphils has changed. Sciphil Two, Zach Flynn, has no blood relation to Ayana Dee. Daniel Chandler has no blood relation to Juliette

Dubois. He does, however, have a family tie with Sciphil Nine, Pete Chandler. And with you, Tadgh."

Tadgh nodded. "As Sciphil Seven, I have no family tie with Ralph Durant. But I do have a blood tie with Ciaran."

Jo nodded and said, "So the Sciphil Four line of succession is a mumbo jumbo."

"I was wondering why Hoyt Flanagan didn't appoint a human successor for the Sciphil Four position," Tadgh said. "And why other Eudaizian Sciphils didn't appoint their relations. They have family ties in Eudaiz, like we humans."

Jo stood up and paced back and forth. "When Kyle kidnapped me on Earth, he had an entire army working for him," she said. She turned and looked at Tadgh. "Wait a second. All Sciphil Fours before me didn't have blood ties. They were all Eudaizian...born from boxes. I want their birth records, Ted."

"Unfortunately, you don't have access to that information."

"Ahhh... so who does?" Jo snarled.

"Ciaran," Tadgh said before the robot could reply.

"All right," Jo muttered and engaged her computer system to create a holocast to Ciaran's residence. "District Four. Tower Four. Me—Sciphil Four. Now there are four Eudaizians in this line of Sciphil succession," she said.

Tadgh nodded. "Yes, there's a pattern. But of what? What would make a pattern of four? Four gods? Four elements? Like metal, water, fire, and earth?"

She chuckled. "Or simply the four points of a square. But all of these Eudaizian Sciphils are dead now. So that makes them dead squares."

The computer monitor blinked a couple of times, and then the screen went blank.

"What the hell?" Jo looked at the monitor.

"Look out!" Tadgh shouted and dove at her. He hit her so hard they both fell to the floor.

In front of them, the computer exploded.

CHAPTER 2

Madeline stormed into the control room and saw that Ciaran had just finished giving instructions to staff and had programmed a couple of bug-like robots. He raised a hand to gesture her to wait. Once the staff had cleared the room, he turned toward her.

"Jo and Tadgh are fine." He approached her and rubbed his thumb on the dimple on her left cheek.

Madeline exhaled, releasing a ton of anxiety. Her psychic ability had decided to balk when she'd needed it the most. Ciaran kissed her. He always did that—before she could rant, ask questions, or complain about anything. The next thing she knew, she'd almost forgotten what she had stormed in here for.

"Fine? As in not dead? Free from injuries?"

He smiled. "Jo and Tadgh were thrown into a dimensional hole as a result of the explosion. But Jo managed to shoot a message back here before the hole closed. The message said they were both okay. She'll get back to us when she can locate their physical position."

"Are you sure she can?"

He nodded. "I am. And they're free from injury—that's the most important thing. I can't say the same about Jo's robot, however."

Madeline narrowed her eyes. "Wait...how did Jo's home robot get to your control room?"

"I picked him up and transported him here."

"You've been to Sciphil Four's residence and back?"

He nodded and smiled. "I'm efficient."

Madeline sighed and said nothing. She was busy asking their own home robot, Robert, to teach her to use the inter-universal communicator so that she could call the Daimon Gate directly to check on the children.

He rubbed his thumb on her chin. "I have something to discuss with you, First Councillor."

Damn it! Her hormones were always stirred up whenever he called her First Councillor. Maybe it was because of the way he said it. Maybe his British accent was what turned her on. She cleared her throat. "Sure."

He smiled again. "Promise me you won't get upset."

She narrowed her eyes. "Jo was really injured?"

He shook his head.

"Tadgh?"

He shook his head again.

"You?"

"Promise me!"

"Okay, I promise."

He nodded. "I was able to retrieve the last search function Jo performed on the robot before the explosion. And the information—or rather, what I can deduce from it—warranted some attention."

She paced the room. Her psychic feelings started to creep in, none of them good.

Ciaran grabbed her shoulders, holding her still. He looked into her eyes. "Jo thinks someone related to the succession line of the Sciphil Four position is planning to do something catastrophic before—or maybe on—the day of my coronation. And it has something to do with Dead Squares because when she said the words, her computer system exploded."

When it came to computers, Madeline didn't need to ask Ciaran or Jo whether they were sure about their speculations. They were usually right, at least most of the time. She sighed and nodded.

Ciaran continued, "It could be anything. It could be a chess move...or a location. Jo thinks it might have something to do with the way children are born in Eudaiz. I've checked the profiles of all four Eudaizian Sciphils. All were born in District Four. And I don't think the profiles stored in the system are authentic."

"So what's the part you think I'd be upset about?"

He sighed. "I'm afraid it could get a bit more complicated. I think it has to do with the number four. Considering the four Eudaizian Sciphils,

Kyle Wolf was number four. That was why he was so ambitious. He wanted to be king of Eudaiz."

"And that's why he ended up dead," she said.

Ciaran nodded. "Because Kyle wasn't meant to be king. Whoever planned the ennead codes either wants to be king or wants to build the rightful king for Eudaiz. Judging by how someone tried to pry information out of my mind and the way we were attacked before, I think it has something to do with children born in the Red Stage of the Daimon Gate."

"So it might have something to do with you and our children," Madeline said.

"Three of us, and maybe one more," Ciaran said. "If what Moira claimed is true—that she had a daughter conceived during the Red Stage of the Daimon Gate, and her daughter is alive in Xiilok, her daughter is number four."

"So you think it might have something to do with Moira?"

Ciaran nodded. "And that's the upsetting part for you. I know you sympathize with her situation. And given she's my ancestor, I should be more sympathetic. But I think that not only does Moira want to build super soldiers to find her daughter, she also wants her daughter in the king Sciphil position." He turned and looked into her eyes. "You know I don't care whether I'm king or not. But I'm a firm believer of nurture over nature. If Moira's daughter was raised in Xiilok—the land of the multiversal outlaws—and was brought up by her captor, a traitor of Eudaiz, then she's not fit to be the queen of Eudaiz."

"Ciaran."

"Yes, First Councillor."

This time, his First Councillor sounded cold. He spoke it almost like a reminder that she held a position with great responsibilities, and all personal matters and feelings must be set aside. "What do you want me to do, Ciaran?"

"Break your promise with Moira. We will not help her find her daughter."

She stared at Ciaran. "You remember that our children were born using Moira's technology. You can prevent her from having direct contact with the children, but there's nothing to stop her from remotely controlling the birth chamber."

"You don't have to tell her anything before we have a chance to secure our children."

"Let me get this straight. You want me to not only break my promise with that poor woman but also lie to her. Okay. Fine and dandy. I'll do that for the sake of my children. But when push comes to shove, when Moira needs an answer, I will not upset her."

"I told you we can secure the children. And they're *our* children by the way."

"No, Ciaran. If you could have taken our children out of those boxes—before they hatched—you would have done so already. So as long as our children's lives are in Moira's hands, I refuse to upset her."

"Our children aren't chickens. They don't hatch. And I told you I would get them out of those boxes," Ciaran growled. "Be patient. Make yourself unavailable to Moira. That way, she won't ask you questions, and you don't have to lie. That is, if you insist on holding your moral ground with her."

She snarled back, "I know you have a universe on your shoulders, and I realize you take your responsibility seriously. Unlike a petulant councillor like me."

"That's not what I said."

"It's what you implied. Keep your moral ground, and stay up there on your high horse. Take care of your universe. But I am a mother. My children will always be my top priority. They are not yet safe and sound in my arms, so there is nothing you can say or do that will change my mind. Do your best, and keep Moira away from me." She strode out of the room, breaking her promise to him.

She was royally upset.

CHAPTER 3

The cold breeze seeped up from the ground and absorbed into her fragile skin. Jo shuddered. She couldn't tell whether she was still in Eudaiz or had been transported into another dimension. But she didn't care for the eeriness around her at the moment. It reminded her of her darkest days in New York—the ones she didn't care to remember and had never told anyone about, including her best friend, Madeline.

She glanced around. Tadgh was nowhere to be found. She didn't have Madeline's psychic abilities, but she had a feeling he was alive and looking for her.

He was her second chance in life, and she wasn't about to take their relationship for granted. She promised herself when she found him that she would make more of an effort to make their relationship easier. She couldn't keep letting her past haunt the most beautiful thing happening in her in life.

From the corner of her eye, she saw the shape of something moving in the dark.

"Who's that?" she shouted and reached her hand out for her gun only to discover she didn't have it. *Damn it*, she cursed silently. Because she had been working with a computer in her control room before being plunged down into this dark hole, she hadn't had any weapons with her. She hadn't been prepared.

The shadow grew larger and wriggled toward her.

"Don't come near me. I'll hurt you!" she shouted again, having no idea yet how she intended to hurt a ten-foot-tall, human-shaped shadow. The air around her thickened, and the space seemed to close in on her. The ground lifted up and lowered as if it was breathing, and a small amount of liquid oozed out on the surface from seemingly nowhere. It seemed as if the air around her had liquified and materialized, acting as a curtain that the shadow was pushing against.

Jo turned around to run. It was the most sensible solution given the circumstances. Her face smashed into a jelly-like wall, and she felt her head bounce backward. She squinted and saw a light that seemed to come from her right-hand side, via something that shaped like the entrance to a cave. The entrance was closing. She wasn't in a hole—she was in a cave. The air smelled awful. The shadow in front of her became more prominent and seemed to be coming closer. The good part was that it was getting smaller as it closed in.

Jo realized it had looked gigantic before because of the distance and the light distortion. The ground beneath her rose and fell, rose and fell.

The shadow came right up to the jelly-like wall and was separated from her by only the thin layer of a damp tissue. It clawed and pushed at the curtain as if trying to find its way out—or in.

Jo glanced again at the closing mouth of the cave. It was time for her to flee. As soon as she turned, she heard the shadow calling her name.

"What the hell? Who's that?" she asked.

The sharp tip of an object poked at the gelatinous curtain from the other side, and a dagger slipped through, slicing it open. The curtain parted to reveal Madeline, covered in a slimy substance. Jo heard moaning from somewhere deep inside the cave. Hot, putrid air pumped out in waves.

"Madeline!" Jo exclaimed.

Madeline looked at the rising and falling ground where Jo was standing and tried to maintain her balance. She glanced to the far end of the cave on her left and then to the closing cave mouth on her right.

"Is this place alive?" Madeline asked.

Jo realized that Madeline might be right. It looked like they were in the mouth of a living creature, and it felt as if the creature was either going to spit them out or swallow them. Personally, she preferred the former.

CHAPTER 4

"Jo!" Tadgh called out, cursing under his breath. They had been thrown into a black hole after the computer in her control room exploded. As soon as they got to their feet, Jo had tried to message Ciaran. Before she could do anything further, he grabbed her and kissed her, and then they were thrown away for a second time. All he had now was the lingering sweet taste of her lips on his, but Jo was nowhere to be found.

He thought they were going to die. He was no psychic, but his unfortunate connection with Kyle had given him an unwanted talent that allowed him to read the emotions of Kyle's victims. Jo had been one of them, and thus he could live and breathe her emotions. The bad news was that whatever she dealt with hit him with an earth-shattering magnitude.

Kyle was dead. He was free of that connection. But he still could read a part of Jo's emotions, and he liked it that way. After Jo messaged Ciaran, he saw fear in her mind. Fear shouldn't be a part of her emotional portfolio as far as Tadgh was concerned. He loved her because of her fearlessness. He admired her tenacious approach to life. Her qualities made up for what he lacked. Seeing fear in Jo left him feeling hopeless. He would not allow that to happen.

Tadgh surveyed his surroundings.

The fear clawed at him now.

Khanuilay.

The scenery around him had an odd resemblance to the Khanuilay camp in Black Rock, where hundred of Eudaizians had been captured and ended up sacrificing themselves to buy himself and Ciaran time to escape. It was the camp that Libby was from. Her soul was still locked in a stone that he kept in his drawer to remind himself that life had been lost for him to be in a position to serve Eudaiz. It reminded him that he was a man with larger-than-life responsibilities—a concept he found difficult to swallow.

But this place didn't look exactly like the camp he had been to with Ciaran. The camp had been a mocked-up area within Black Rock to simulate the real Khanuilay in District One. He had never had a chance to find out the true purpose of the camp before everyone involved was killed, but he remembered vividly how close he had been to giving an incorrect command, a command for the real Khanuilay in District One to be destroyed. If that had happened, he would have collapsed Eudaiz.

It was Ciaran who had stopped him. Tadgh sighed. Where would he be—what would he be—without his brother?

Earth had become a part of his past. Eudaiz was his future. He owed people here his life.

"Jo!" Tadgh called again and charged faster toward the hill.

An aura blasted at his senses now. He shook his head. If this was Black Rock, he knew how to handle these creatures. He checked for his guns and daggers and was relieved—his weapons were still with him even after all of the dimensional travel. Then he remembered that Jo wouldn't have a weapon with her. The fear of that clawed at him.

In a worst case scenario—if what he was sensing now was sorcery, the kind that the man at the creek in Xiilok had used on Ciaran—even with him and Jo together, with or without their weapons, they would be in serious trouble.

Behind him, the sand whirled up and formed the shape of a scorpion with eight claws reaching out in multiple directions. The presence of the creature created a pressure in the air. Tadgh turned around. Seeing the creature, he reached for his guns.

CHAPTER 5

Via the closing cave mouth, they could see a dimly lit landscape. Jo darted over to help Madeline untangle herself from a web of something that looked like saliva. As soon as Madeline was free from the web, Jo shouted, "Run!"

They didn't need to. The hot air seemed to move inward then outward. The ground vibrated. There was the sound of something like a train approaching on loose tracks. Then a jet of hot air and water shot Madeline and Jo outside the cave. They rolled across the soft grassy ground then scrambled to their feet.

"Are you okay, Madeline?" Jo asked.

"Yes. You?"

"Still in one piece, I think. How did you get here?"

"In a capsule. Robert programmed it for me, and I set it to take me to where I sensed you were. Tadgh isn't in there, is he?"

"No. We were pulled apart really hard on the second attack. He didn't end up here with me, but hopefully he's in the same dimension. We'll need a capsule to find him. Where did you park?"

"I didn't exactly park. The capsule just landed." Madeline glanced toward the mouth of the cave.

"Oh, it took you into that mouth," Jo said. The mouth had closed, revealing the face of an old man. The face was carved into the stone and was as big as the side of the small hill. The eyes of the stone man opened. He blinked at Madeline and Jo and then winced.

"My capsule must still be in his mouth," Madeline said.

"He's going to sneeze again—get down!" Jo shouted.

They dropped to the ground.

A sneezing sound rumbled above them like thunder. A burst of hot air shot out along with something liquid, which they knew now to be saliva. Pieces of metal rained to the ground around them.

"I'm guessing this used to be my capsule," Madeline said.

"As long as he didn't chew us up, he can have the capsule."

They stood up to look at the stone face which appeared to have recovered from its sneezing frenzy. Jo looked in disgust at her clothes, which were soaked through with sticky saliva.

"Who are you?" Madeline asked.

"I'm a stone observer."

"That's *what* you are not *who* you are," Jo said.

"We don't have names. We live on mountains and hillsides. We listen, we watch, and we tell stories."

"Where are we?" Madeline asked.

"Xiilok."

"Xiilok is an entire universe! Could you be a bit more precise?" Jo asked irritably.

"As you can see, I'm stuck on the side of a hill. I've been here since I was only a small lump of dirt. The only thing I know is that I am still within this dimension, in Xiilok."

"He's right, Jo. Xiilok is a land of illusion and multiversal outlaws. Unless you're a Xiilok citizen, you can't see the forever changing landscape," Madeline said. She turned toward the stone observer. "We have another companion. Have you seen him?"

"Yes, he was just on the other side of me."

"The other side of the hill? Does he know you're here? Can he see your face? Is he okay?" Jo asked.

"Which question would you like me to answer first?"

"Is he okay?"

"Yes. He was walking around, calling out your name. He can't see my face because he is behind me. But I can hear him."

Jo narrowed her eyes. "How do you know my name?"

"I have listened to stories for a very long time and have heard your stories many times."

"This is creepy. Do you know who I am?" Madeline asked.

"Of course. You're Madeline LeBlanc."

"Right. So what story have you heard about me?" Madeline asked.

"It has to do with your husband and Eudaiz. But I shouldn't tell it in front of a stranger."

"Jo is my best friend. She's not a stranger." Madeline scowled as she sensed a pressure in the air pushing toward her. "Duck!" she yelled out and ducked down. But something sharp hit her right shoulder. "Ow," she grunted and saw that a knife had slashed into her flesh, cutting her deeply. The offending knife lay on the ground. When she whirled around, she saw a man in military uniform.

As quick as a cat, Jo picked up the knife and charged at the soldier. She slashed at his abdomen. Plastic and wire poured out from the cut Jo had made.

"Attacking from behind is an insult to men in the multiverse," Jo said as the robot vanished. She stepped back and asked, "How's your injury, Madeline?"

"Just a flesh wound," Madeline said, then yelled, "Behind you!"

But it was too late. Three soldiers emerged from the sand right behind Jo. One of them gave her a hard kick and sent her flying over into Madeline. Both of them fell to the ground.

As they scrambled to their feet, the soldiers drew long swords and charged at them. These were a lot more vicious than the one Jo had just killed. Madeline recalled Ciaran mentioning that mechanical weapons wouldn't work in Xiilok because of the unstable properties in the dimension. But even with swords, she wasn't sure she and Jo had any chance against these gigantic robotic soldiers.

The soldiers advanced.

"We should run," Madeline said through her teeth.

"Where to?" Jo asked and looked around. Behind them was a fast moving creek, and it was too foggy for her to see what was on the other side. "What if there's an army over there? I'd rather fight the three of them here than an army over there."

"Okay, take this," Madeline said and gave Jo one of her paired daggers.

They withdrew slightly as the soldiers advanced. The howling wind intensified, tangling their hair and blowing sand into their eyes. They heard the stone observer sigh and grumble something that sounded like his condolences.

CHAPTER 6

Ciaran slammed his palm onto the control panel and got no response. He had never experienced such fear in his life. The system reported that the capsule Madeline had requested had vanished from the radar.

He had no way to trace her. No way to communicate. He wasn't the psychic one in this relationship. If there was to be any kind of psychic communication, she would have to initiate it. And he had heard nothing from her for an entire unit of Eudaizian time.

He thought of what he had last said to her but immediately brushed the thought away. That sort of thinking was accepting defeat. He would never give up when it came to Madeline or their children.

He evaluated the situation again. She was mad at him because he had asked her to dishonor her promise to Moira and risk their children's lives. He hadn't meant to say it that way, but that's how it had come out. She had walked away and had requested the capsule, asking their home robot to program it for her. The log in the system suggested that she'd wanted an open destination.

He knew her all too well. She had gone to search for Jo and Tadgh using her psychic ability. Her sense of their presence would be her guide. That was why when the capsule disappeared from the radar, there was no log of her journey.

Ciaran engaged the communication channel. At the other end of the line, Sizx's voice spoke up, "Yes, Ciaran?"

"Do you have any new information for me, Sizx?"

"Unfortunately, no. I have searched every route the capsule could travel in Eudaiz—twice. Our systems wouldn't miss anything. Is there anything else you can think of that I could use to track her capsule? Just give me the direction, and I will search."

Ciaran stared at Sizx's image on the monitor. She looked at him with concern. "How could I be that stupid?" he muttered to himself. "Thank you, Sizx. That will be all for today," he said and turned on his heel, hurrying out of the control room.

***

The sandy wind distorted Jo and Madeline's vision. But they knew the three gigantic sand creatures in front of them were no illusion. They were as real as the three swords they carried— swords that must weigh a ton by the bulky look of the blades.

Withdrawing and speaking between her teeth so the creatures wouldn't hear, Madeline said, "I think running is a bad idea. If they throw those swords at us, they'll do a lot more damage than the small cut on my shoulder."

"Agreed. Do you think we can duck and run between their legs toward the stone observer? They don't look as if they can move very fast."

Madeline looked at Jo, arching an eyebrow.

"Damn," Jo cursed. Jo was five foot two and had used body sensor technology to perform a lot of combat movements in the days when she had designed fight games. Madeline was five foot eight. She was quick and agile, but she was much taller than Jo. There was no way she could do what Jo had just suggested.

The sand creatures advanced.

Madeline and Jo backed further away, toward the creek behind them. The air grew colder and creepier by the second. Jo pushed Madeline behind her back.

"You're not my bodyguard, Jo," Madeline growled.

"You shouldn't have come here," Jo said. "I can do a lot of things. But if anything happened to you, I wouldn't know what to do with Ciaran and your children. How could Ciaran let you go off in a capsule alone?"

"I had a fight with him—and before you say anything, he's not always right."

Jo rolled her eyes. "Of course not. Well, what do you think? Should we go ahead and do our best against these sand creatures?"

Madeline nodded, but by the look on her face, Jo knew her best friend wasn't confident about their chances. Jo didn't like the aura of the area. It wouldn't have surprised her to see space creatures coming at them in all directions from thin air.

Then from the corner of her eye, Jo saw Tadgh charging at the sand creatures from behind. He pulled out his guns.

"No!" Jo yelled, but it was too late. Tadgh fired. The laser beams bent and whirled in a circle, shooting off into the stone observer's face. They heard something that sounded like a moan.

After seeing the effect of the beams, Tadgh stopped shooting. But the shots had caught the sand creatures' attention. They turned around and set their sights on Tadgh.

"Go to hell!" Jo yelled. She pulled her dagger and charged at the creatures' backs.

Madeline followed suit, stabbing her knife blade deep into the lower back of one of the creatures. Jo, who couldn't reach as high, ended up stabbing into the ass of another. The holes they had opened in the creatures were filling in with sand from their bodies. The two creatures growled and turned back to them. The third one continued to advance on Tadgh.

The stone observer sighed and said, "Send them back to where they came from."

"How?" Madeline asked.

Jo looked at Tadgh. They both looked at the stone observer and, at the same time, said, "Dead squares."

The ground in front of them exploded.

CHAPTER 7

The hole in the ground was humongous as if the explosion had dug a tunnel from one dimension to another. Jo peeked over the edge, but Tadgh pulled her back from behind, threw her over his shoulder, and carried her away. He didn't like the feel of this place. The hillside was eerie. As much as he loved the fun and excitement of travel on Earth, being in this place didn't strike him as either adventurous or intriguing. It was just plain spooky.

"Put me down," Jo snarled.

Tadgh winced. "We have to get away from that rancid hole."

"It's not the hole that smells—it's us, Tadgh," Madeline said and sniffed at her clothes. "We've just been inside the mouth of that—"

They looked up and saw that the explosion had created a crack in the ground which ran toward the bottom of the hill. Half of the stone observer's face had collapsed into the crack. The one eye he had left was closed.

"Oh no! We've killed him," Tadgh said.

He was still angry that Madeline and Jo had attacked the creatures to protect him. He may not have been able to handle the creatures in hand to hand combat, but he could always figure a way out. The monsters hadn't looked very intelligent or dangerous. They were just big.

He swallowed hard, looking up at what was left of the stone observer. It looked like a fallen statue of a deity who had once guarded the gates between heaven and hell. Tadgh approached the stone man.

"I'm so sorry," Tadgh said but jumped back and gasped when the one eye opened.

"Don't worry, you didn't kill me. But it will take a very long time for me to build up the other half of my face again."

Jo and Madeline approached. "What do you know about the command? How did you know it would send the creatures back to the sand?" Jo asked.

"I know that these creatures can only be brought forth by a command. But I don't know what that command is," the stone observer answered cryptically.

"You said this is Xiilok. Is there a way we can get back to where we came from without a capsule?" Madeline asked.

"I don't know, Madeline. Can't your people track your vehicle?"

"They could, but you chewed up her capsule!" Jo yelled.

"You are the ones who flew into my mouth. I did my best not to grind you up accidentally. But that object hit my tooth and broke. There was nothing I could do about it. But there's something still stuck between my teeth. I think a part of your flying egg is still there, and it's leaking something very distasteful." The stone observer winced.

"It might be the motherboard. I'm going to go in and get it," Jo said and approached the mouth.

"No, I'll do it." Tadgh pulled her back. He approached the mouth and grimaced at the stench of the hot air that blew out of the dark, black cave. He stepped reluctantly over the front teeth and entered.

Inside the mouth, rows and rows of ivory teeth grew along the side. "Why in the world do you need so many teeth? What could you possibly be eating?" he mumbled.

"I don't eat," the stone man responded. "What you're looking for is between two teeth toward the back of my right jaw."

Tadgh grunted a thank you and walked toward the rear of the stone man's mouth on ground that continuously rose and fell. He guessed it was the stone observer's tongue. The thought disgusted him, so he tried to brush it away and concentrate on the task at hand. He saw the square black motherboard stuck between the teeth just as the observer had said. Tadgh looked back toward the outside of the cave and saw the mouth closing.

"Hey! You're not going to swallow me, are you?"

"Don't worry—I'll open my mouth when you need to exit." The voice came from deep inside the cave-like tunnel that Tadgh assumed was the throat.

"Okay, how about letting me out now?" Tadgh said as he started to pull at the motherboard. It slipped easily out of the gap between the two teeth. He hoped it wasn't damaged. When he turned around, he saw that the mouth of the cave still hadn't opened yet. "Do I need to say open sesame?" he snapped.

"I don't know what you mean. But I have something to negotiate with you."

"Sure, but we can certainly do it outside."

"Tadgh LeBlanc, I can give you magic."

Tadgh laughed. "No, thank you. I don't feel the need to turn a rabbit into a dove."

"That's a trick, not magic. My magic is a paranormal phenomenon that even your brother couldn't explain with science."

"I'm still not interested. Now can you please open your mouth, or do I have to dig my way out?" Tadgh pulled his dagger threateningly.

"Your brother was born the best being in the cosmos in many respects, but he has a lot of weaknesses."

"That's not breaking news. That's why I'm here to help."

"One of Ciaran's major drawbacks is magic. It isn't a matter of belief. He will eventually come to terms with the paranormal worlds. But he has no way of creating or using paranormal abilities. And unfortunately, one of his most notorious enemies practices magic and has a distinct advantage over Ciaran. If you want to help your brother, this is your chance."

Tadgh shifted his stance to get his balance on the uneven ground. "Why me?" he asked.

"Because you are a natural mathematical genius. Together, you and Ciaran will be able to alter dimensional travel in the cosmos. You will be able to alter time and space."

Tadgh grinned. "Now all of a sudden you're a fortune-teller? Let's assume what you're saying is true. That would mean we will be able to change time and space in the cosmos in the future *without* your magic. So why would I listen to your offer now?"

"Because that's only one version of reality. Your enemy—a man with a pool of abilities gathered through hundreds of years of Earth time and a man who walks across boundaries between the multiverse and the paranormal worlds—desires a different version of reality. And in that version, I don't see you brothers surviving."

"Who's that man?"

"I don't know. I saw the shadow of him only once when he created the command that caused all the explosions and sent you here. But all creatures in the cosmos know of him. They call him Master."

Tadgh contemplated. He almost laughed at the thought of having magical abilities, but he composed himself. "What sort of magic can you give me?"

"Dematerialization in a short period of time."

"That doesn't sound much like magic. And how short a period of time are you talking about? Will I get all of my..." Tadgh held the motherboard with one hand and gestured up and down his body with it as he spoke "...natural properties back after I rematerialize?"

"The duration of dematerialization will vary depending on your energy and physical strength at the time you use it. When you're new to it, the safest and shortest time is equivalent to thirty seconds Earth time. And yes, you will be the same both before and after dematerialization."

"How many creatures in the cosmos have this ability?"

"Not many. The ones with advanced skills can materialize and dematerialize specific parts of their bodies. Some can also turn into other creatures, other people, or weapons. But at a basic level, you can dematerialize for only thirty seconds and can't doing anything during the process."

"That doesn't sound very appealing," Tadgh muttered. But he did think the ability would come in handy at some point. And he was willing to do whatever it took to help Ciaran. "All right. What is this going to cost me? What do you want in return?"

"If you agree to accept it, dip your hand into the well back where you found your piece of equipment."

Tadgh glanced behind him at a tooth filled with a boiling blue liquid. "That's a cavity, not a well. Don't you know how disgusting that is? Tell me exactly what I have to do in return for this magic."

"I need a promise from you that you will liberate Xiilok."

Tadgh let out a short laugh. "Xiilok is a universe of multiversal outlaws. It's not governed by anyone. Man, you can't get more liberation than that! Ciaran is a better person to handle this sort of deal."

"Do you think I can get your brother into my mouth?"

Tadgh chuckled. "No, he's not an idiot."

"And neither are you, Tadgh. Xiilok needs even more help than Eudaiz does. If you care, Ciaran will care."

"Well, if that's all you need, I'll talk to Ciaran."

"I don't have that kind of time. I need a promise from you. Now."

"What do you mean?"

"I've been waiting for many years. An opportunity like this may never come again."

"I said I would talk to Ciaran," Tadgh said and turned on his heel, heading toward the exit which was still shut.

"I need you to say you will take the magic and promise to help liberate Xiilok."

Tadgh narrowed his eyes. "What is it that you aren't telling me? I won't make a deal if I'm not sure about it. I'm not getting my brother tangled in whatever shit you're involved with."

"I'm collapsing. There's no time to explain."

"You told me the explosion didn't kill you."

"If I told you I was collapsing, would you have come in here? Xiilok used to be a happy universe, just like Eudaiz. There were millions of families, Tadgh. I know it's not your business. And I know it will be difficult and dangerous to save them. But it is possible for you. And impossible for me."

"Who are you, really?"

"I am—" The rumbling noise of collapsing sand hills echoed from deep inside the mouth. "It's too late... You don't have to promise me anything. I am going to let you out now. Will you take the magic?"

"Okay...I'll accept it."

"Thank you. I was once the prince of Xiilok. The key to saving Xiilok is at the bottom of the well."

And that was all Tadgh heard before a wave of hot red fumes shot out from deep inside the cave. They blanketed his body, and he felt every cell in his body burn as the darkness claimed him.

CHAPTER 8

Madeline looked at the empty space where the hillside used to be. The stone observer had spat out Tadgh the way he had Jo and her, and then his face crumbled away into a mound of sand and dirt and rocks. He must have been thousands of years old.

"No!" Jo's cry sent her scrambling back to where Tadgh lay on the ground, glowing red.

The look on Jo's face was heartrending. Madeline's best friend hadn't realized how much she loved Tadgh. She had never admitted it and had never shown too much affection. She had used the fact that Kyle had raped her and she would never be good enough for Tadgh as an excuse. One day, Madeline would probe the heck out of her friend for the real reason.

Madeline crouched to check Tadgh's pulse. Jo grabbed her hand and pulled her back so hard that that both fell backward to the ground. Jo's voice was choked with tears. "Don't touch him. My hand went right through him...through his body. He...he's disintegrating..." Then she just broke down and cried. Madeline had never seen her so defeated.

"Jo, it's okay."

"No, it's not. He's dying."

"No, I'm not sensing his death. And I'm psychic, remember?"

There was a hum in the air as a rail-free capsule zoomed over, hovered, and landed. From inside the capsule, Ciaran darted out. His eyes zeroed in on Tadgh as he rushed over. He was too fast for Madeline to do or say anything to stop him. He reached instinctively to check Tadgh's pulse. His hand went right through Tadgh's wrist. Ciaran jerked back. And just like Jo, the look on his face broke Madeline's heart. He said nothing. He stood up and stood in place, looking as if he had no idea what to do. In the meantime, Tadgh's body had become fifty percent transparent.

"Ciaran, I'm not sensing his death. He's alive. Do you hear me, Ciaran?" Madeline caressed his face, trying to get him to look at her. It didn't work. He wasn't listening. She was a psychic and the First Councillor of Eudaiz. For the multiverse's sake, she had to do something. She whirled around, pacing back and forth while Ciaran and Jo stared at Tadgh's rapidly disappearing body.

Madeline looked at Tadgh. She still wasn't sensing his death. And that meant that she should be able to communicate with him in whatever dimension he was at the moment. She wasn't just a psychic—she was a mind tracker. She closed her eyes and opened her communication channel to Tadgh.

Empty and dark space. That was what she saw. "Come on. Give me a signal. A blue dot. Come on, Tadgh," she muttered.

"Madeline," Tadgh called from behind, making her jump out of her skin. She must have yelped out loud because Ciaran and Jo turned and looked at her. Madeline turned around and saw Tadgh standing there with a red halo around his body. Wait—she had just seen Ciaran and Jo. In *this* reality. But they didn't look as if they had seen Tadgh behind her. And the Tadgh lying on the ground was still there—and about ninety-five percent transparent.

Should she respond to the Tadgh behind her? she asked herself. Probably not a good idea before she figured out what was going on. Madeline looked at the standing Tadgh and channeled her questions to his mind. "What's going on Tadgh?"

"I'm not dying. Can you tell Ciaran and Jo? I hate seeing the look on their faces."

"You have to give me more than that. I already told them you're not dying. But as you can see, it didn't work."

"The stone observer put something into me. He called it magic, but I don't know what it was. In principle, I can dematerialize for about thirty seconds and then put myself back together. This is the first time I've done it, so it might take a little longer. Apparently, I have to practice. At the moment, I..." Tadgh's image flickered, and his voice started to crack. "I can't control it..."

Madeline glanced at Tadgh lying on the ground and saw that his body had completely disappeared. Jo cried and flew into Ciaran's arms.

Madeline turned around to find that the Tadgh behind her had disappeared as well. "Tadgh!" she whispered.

"He's gone," Jo said.

They heard a rumbling in the distance. From around the side of a low hill, a line of sand creatures appeared. Madeline knew now that they were just big and stupid soldiers. But Ciaran turned and saw them. His eyes were filled with rage at the thought that his brother was dead. Madeline had never seen his eyes so dark. He stepped in front of her and Jo and gazed at the line of sand creatures. They were about to experience a painful and merciless death.

Ciaran concentrated. In a short moment, his blade of rage appeared like a gigantic spinning fan, descending on the creatures. He hit them so hard that the blade dug into the ground, and soon the hole in front of them looked like a copy of the Grand Canyon. In no time, there was nothing left of the creatures. But the supernatural blade didn't come for free. It cost Ciaran energy. He staggered back but regained his stance quickly.

It hadn't been necessary to hit the creatures so hard. But Madeline knew he had been raging mad at the moment it happened. It had been out of his control.

"Let's go!" he said to Madeline and Jo.

"You can't leave Tadgh here," Madeline said.

"Madeline, he's not here... He..." Ciaran trailed off when he saw a shade of Tadgh's body reappear. Madeline jumped on the opportunity. "I told you—Tadgh wasn't dying. If you two would only listen to me—my psychic mind can see Tadgh and communicate with him."

Ciaran turned toward Madeline. "I'm listening, First Councillor!"

Judging by the look on Ciaran's face, Madeline knew he had guessed what was going on. He crouched next to Tadgh's reforming body. "He can dematerialize."

"You know what, Ciaran, sometimes it would be nice if you didn't know everything." Madeline scowled.

He approached and touched her dimple and smiled. "I don't know magic!"

Jo sat down next to Tadgh and waited patiently.

A sudden, strange energy hit Madeline in waves. The waves rose and fell, blanketing the entire area. She frowned, and Ciaran immediately caught the signals. Tadgh's materialization process halted at fifty percent. His haloed other half darted over to stand next to Madeline.

"A creature is nearby. I don't know what it's trying to do," Tadgh said.

Madeline didn't want to say anything to Ciaran. She didn't know what the creature was capable of or whether it could intercept her psychic channel, but it seemed far safer than saying it out loud. She held Ciaran's hand and looked into his eyes.

"Ciaran, nod if you can hear me," Madeline said in her mind.

He nodded slightly.

"There's a creature—"

She hadn't finished her sentence when Ciaran jerked his body back as a sharp object sliced open the front of his vest and cut into his flesh. He grabbed at the wound, and blood seeped out from the gaps between his fingers.

CHAPTER 9

In a mansion in Xiilok, he strode back and forth, striking any objects in his way. This entire multiverse should be at his feet. Creatures feared him. Soldiers fell dead just by hearing his name. They called him Master for a reason. It meant Master of the multiverse. Master of all things. He had developed way beyond common sorcery. Beyond the realm of magic and science. Beyond what feeble human brains could comprehend.

What did the LeBlancs have that he didn't? Except for a lot of luck, they had nothing. And now that luck threatened what belonged to him. He had worked hard. He had invested everything in this. He would never accept defeat because of the blind luck of the LeBlanc brothers.

His communicator beeped, and a voice came through a robotic filter. "Master, I have located the LeBlancs and have sent our best soldiers."

"I know. What's new?" he snarled.

"I'd like to confirm that you want them dead."

"Yes. And painfully. Get my people in Eudaiz ready. As soon as these bad boys are dead, message me, and I'll execute the Dead Squares to replace their power."

"Are you sure, Master?"

He paused and stared at the speaker. "Are you questioning my order?"

"No, Master. My apologies. I just want to make sure you're not rushing. The coronation is just days away—"

He shouted at the speaker, "Don't you dare question me! Do what I said. It's your job to do what I tell you."

Silence.

He sighed and took some time to compose himself. Then he said, "It was very brave of you to oppose my order."

"It's my life mission to see you follow your plan to fruition."

He nodded and then realized the person at the other end couldn't see his nod. He cleared his throat. "All right..."

***

"Get behind me," Ciaran said and pulled at Madeline and Jo. It was unacceptable for the two women he cared about to protect him. He glanced over to Tadgh's body—it was still at fifty percent in the materialization process. "Get back into your form, Tadgh. If you think hanging around at fifty percent body mass is going to help me, you're sadly mistaken."

He felt a slight density in the air and the pressure of something pushing forward. He couldn't send out the blade of fury because he wasn't sure where Tadgh was standing and what would happen if he hit him by accident in half materialized form. Instinctively, he blocked where he felt a blow would come from and got it right. He followed by shoving his dagger into whatever stood in front of him, and he heard a howl of pain.

It wasn't human. It was a space creature with limited dematerialization capability. He could handle this one. The problem was that he didn't know how many there were. He glanced at Tadgh's body and saw it had started to materialize more. His stubborn brother knew when it was important to follow his older brother's orders.

There was more pressure building in the air. More grumbling as space creatures moved in on him. He put pressure on his bleeding wound. The blood ran down his hand and fingers and dripped to the ground. The injury was quite bad, he thought. If he sent out a blade now in the general direction of the coming creatures, it would cost him a lot of energy, and he wouldn't be standing for long. If he could see exactly where the coming creatures were, he could send the blade right at them. His energy level wouldn't allow him to shoot randomly.

Tadgh was about eighty percent back. He didn't want to touch Tadgh until he was completely back in his material form. But they needed to make a run for the capsule and leave this place.

"I need to see the creatures. If they're the same kind I fought before in Tower Two, they'll show up in reflective light," Ciaran said.

"I'll run to the capsule and shine the headlight into the mirrors of the capsule. It will reflect the light onto the field," Jo said.

"I'll back you," Madeline said.

"All right. You both be careful," Ciaran said.

"You, too," Madeline said and charged right behind Jo, dagger drawn.

Outside, the pressure was coming even closer. Ciaran knew it wasn't a small group of creatures—it was an army. Tadgh was about ninety-five percent back to normal. Jo and Madeline had entered the capsule and shut the door. Ciaran smiled when he thought of how lucky he was to have these two smart women in his life.

He felt a pinch in his side—a knife of some kind. He said nothing and swung his dagger. He heard a grunt and a howl then a thud. The image of a humanoid lizard glowed in green and then disintegrated into nothing.

From the capsule, the two gigantic rear mirrors popped up and swung to the front, dangling in the front of the capsule. The headlights flashed on, struck the mirrors, and bounced back to the field in front of Ciaran.

His prediction was correct. In front of him wasn't a small group of creatures. It was a large army, silently approaching at the edge of the light.

CHAPTER 10

Madeline glanced outside and saw the army of half-animal, half-robotic creatures approaching Ciaran. It looked as if someone had been trying to create super soldiers, but it hadn't quite worked out as planned. Apart from being super big and ugly, they didn't seem to be able to do much. Tadgh sat up groggily on the ground.

Madeline opened the capsule door and yelled, "Ciaran, can you grab Tadgh and run to the capsule?" Jo was still at the control panel, adjusting the mirror so that it beamed the light onto the moving army.

"I can shoot at them. Ask Ciaran if it's okay if I fire at them," said Jo.

"Can you call him on the communicator? They'll hear me if I yell out."

"They're stupid. They operate on commands. They won't understand what you're saying," Jo shouted.

"Ciaran, Jo wants to shoot at them," Madeline yelled.

Ciaran turned to look at her. He shook his head. Then he said something to Tadgh, who had started to stand up. It was a good two hundred feet between the capsule and where Ciaran was, and she couldn't hear what he was saying. She sneaked outside the door.

"Don't!" said Jo. "Go out there, and you'll be a burden, Madeline. He already has Tadgh to take care of."

"Well, he said no to firing on them. He's going to send out his mind blade, and that'll cost him. Blood is streaming from his wound now."

Jo nodded. "He thinks shooting might make the creatures charge. Good precaution. He'll have to use his mind blade."

***

Outside, Ciaran clutched at the slash on his abdomen and felt a searing pain shooting through his head. His left arm started to go numb. "Can you walk, Tadgh?"

Tadgh nodded. "Can you?"

"Yes, for now." Ciaran turned to look at the army of creatures. He closed his eyes, concentrated for a moment. Then he summoned everything he had left and sent a gigantic spinning blade at them.

Body parts, dirt, and stone flew everywhere. The wind howled, carrying with it the haunting cries of the space creatures as they died. The army disintegrated, going back to the dirt from whence they had come. In a short moment, the hillside and the field returned to its eerie quietness.

Ciaran slumped to the ground.

Tadgh dragged him up to his feet, and they both staggered to the capsule. Madeline grabbed both Ciaran and Tadgh, shoved them hurriedly inside the capsule, and sealed the door. Jo started the engine and hovered above the ground.

Ciaran slid down to the floor and sat leaning against the wall. He wiped the blood that trickled down his nose. Madeline went to the medicine cabinet and pulled out the medical box.

"What was the deal with your dematerialization?" Ciaran asked Tadgh.

Tadgh flopped to the floor, sitting next to Ciaran. "Long story. But the short version is that a gigantic man with a stone face as big as the hillside tricked me into climbing into his mouth. He put something into me, some kind of ability. He called it magic because there's some metaphysical element to it that your science can't explain. So in principle, I can dematerialize for about thirty seconds—as a starter. As you can see, I and all my bodily attachments disintegrated and then reassembled just now."

Ciaran nodded. "It's alchemy—a pseudo-science popular on Earth about five or six hundred years ago." He closed his eyes as fatigue pulled at him. Madeline approached and secured his wound with bandages.

"Where are we going now, Ciaran? The navigator stopped working. I need you, Madeline," Jo called out.

"I need to go to Tower Three and get into my chamber to recharge my energy and fix this injury."

"Roger that. Madeline, you have to guide me. I can't put the capsule into autopilot," Jo said.

Madeline nodded, and she stood up, her eyes shooting back to Ciaran's wound. Her voice shook, "Ciaran!"

He opened his eyes and looked up at her. Seeing the look on her face, he looked down as his wound and saw that the blood seeping out through the bandages had turned black.

CHAPTER 11

Tadgh slammed at the control panel. "Don't leave just yet."

"Ciaran is turning bluer by the second, Tadgh," Madeline said.

Ciaran said, "Don't worry, Madeline. It's not poison. If it were, I would have been dead. We have to make sure leaving is the right move. What are you thinking, Tadgh?"

"The hillside and the fields outside, don't they strike you as something familiar? I think it looks like Khanuilay," Tadgh said.

"The camp that captured the Eudaizians? I thought you blew it up?" asked Jo.

Tadgh paced back and forth. "Yes. But we thought Kyle was the one who had captured them. Turned out Kyle was only a pawn. Whoever did that had bigger plans. And that person, I think, might be the one the stone observer referred to as Ciaran's worst enemy. From what he said, it sounds like this guy knows science *and* magic. If there was a one on one between you and him, I wouldn't put my money on you, Ciaran."

"Is that why the observer gave you the so-called magic? So that you could help me? He wanted us to cheat because manipulating magic and science is the worst an individual can do to the multiverse? What did the stone observer want in return?" Ciaran's voice was weakening by the second.

Madeline crouched next to Ciaran and held his hand. "If he wanted you to cheat to win this battle, then do it. You haven't seen him, but I did. He seemed to be a good man."

Tadgh growled, "I'll do more than cheating. I'll gut that bastard, whoever he is."

"I don't think they tried to gut me before. But they could have. I wasn't prepared," Ciaran said, looking down at his wound, which was still bleeding black.

Jo turned around and said, "This will sound random and totally disgusting. But do you think these creatures tried to take a sample of you? If this area is all about materialization, they might want to turn you into one of them. Or worse, make more of them that look like you?"

"If they sampled me, I can sample them as well. Let's see who can make more out of this," Ciaran muttered. "Can you see if there's anything left of the creatures?"

Madeline peeked out the window. "No, they've completely disintegrated." Then she turned around. "The stone observer is still there, though, in a big lump of dirt. I can take some of him as a sample. Would that help?"

"Yes," Ciaran said.

Madeline grabbed a container from the medicine cabinet, but Tadgh snatched the box out of her hand and said, "I'll go. The stone observer didn't disintegrate completely because he isn't *just* a stone observer. He told me he used to be the prince of Xiilok." Tadgh turned on his heel and charged outside.

He came back shortly with the box filled with gray ashes and an ivory piece of bone.

"Is that a piece of tooth?" Jo winced, looking at the bone.

Tadgh shrugged and said nothing.

"Ciaran said we're going to Tower Three. So let's go," Jo said and headed toward the control panel. Because the navigation was inoperable, Madeline followed to give Jo direction using her psychic ability. She gave Ciaran's hand a slight squeeze before she left.

Tadgh looked at his brother, who was leaning against the wall, eyes closed. "Hang in there for me, will you? The stone observer is some kind of fortune-teller. He told me we're going to be doing great in the future. We'll be a big deal in the cosmos. Changing time and space and all that jazz. As much as I hate to admit it, I guess that ends my dream of going back to Earth to ride an elephant in Africa. I wouldn't want to disappoint the old man."

Ciaran opened his eyes. "I'll make you space elephants."

Tadgh laughed.

***

Their capsule soon landed in front of Tower Three. Tadgh and Madeline flanked Ciaran, their arms around him, helping him approach the gate. Ciaran verified at the control panel. The nine round layers of concrete door slid into place, revealing the entrance. The group entered, and the gate shut immediately behind them.

The central chamber of Tower Three was the grandest of all the towers. It was the king tower after all. The glass chamber with the key stone that held the power of the king stared down at them. Although Ciaran wasn't yet king, his power was already connected to the key stone, and it had healed him once before.

Tadgh and Madeline helped him into the glass chamber. The door sealed after they exited.

Inside the chamber, Ciaran leaned against the control desk, looking at the control panel. A square patch appeared with a text line: "You are injured, Ciaran. Please activate the command for the healing process."

He nodded and raised his left palm. Then he stopped. He could see Tadgh raising his arms in the air in frustration outside the glass chamber. He mimed, "What the fuck?"

Madeline had tears in her eyes, but she said nothing. That was his wife, his First Councillor. She was always the one who understood him.

He approached the glass door and punched the exit button. The door slid open.

"What are you thinking, Ciaran?" Tadgh ranted.

Ciaran wiped away the black blood that trickled down his nose. "The command that triggered all the explosions might have something to do with a square because it's in the wording. But regarding the number four, it's just speculation, isn't it, Jo?"

"Yes, because a square has four corners. And I am Sciphil Four," Jo said.

Ciaran leaned against the wall, taking a deep breath to see if it would give him any more energy. He said, "It might have something to do with four things. But we don't have to count to four from one. What if we start counting from zero? Wouldn't it end up at three? What would be the implications if I activated the operation of the power chamber in Tower Three now?"

"Holy shit," Tadgh muttered, glancing around as if someone had stalked them into the king tower.

CHAPTER 12

Sizx scrambled into her private capsule, pushing Ciaran's home robot, Robert, to a corner. "Stay right there and do not disturb me. Ciaran's in trouble."

"Affirmative. I am here to help."

Sizx slammed at the control panel. "Faster!" she grunted.

"Private capsules can only travel at a limited speed. There is a way you can make it go ten percent faster by optimizing the energy consumption. Would you like me to calculate the optimal usage?" Robert asked.

"I know how fast a private capsule can travel," she snarled.

"Then why did you ask the machine to perform an almost impossible task?"

"Why don't you just shut up? If Ciaran hadn't asked, I wouldn't have come and picked you up. If I knew you talked so much, I would have said no."

"You never say no to Ciaran."

"Excuse me?"

"Based on the records, ninety-nine point nine percent of your responses in conversations with Ciaran are positive."

Sizx narrowed her eyes. "What records?"

"Holocast and official communications records."

Sizx exhaled in relief as she remembered vividly the moment she took her clothes off to offer herself to Ciaran. It wasn't a total failure. It wasn't an outright rejection. He did say yes to her request for a kiss and to allow her essence to absorb into a button of his shirt when she died. It must have been the strangest request he had ever received, but she got a yes.

He was a gentleman. Based on what he had said, she just hadn't come along at the right time. He was taken, and his family left no room in his heart for anyone else. If that conversation had been recorded, she would walk the hall of shame throughout the entire multiverse.

Sizx cleared her throat. "Very well, Robert. Make sure you can do whatever Ciaran is going to ask. His coronation is coming in a few days, and we have no room for error. If there's anything you are unsure about, ask."

"Sizx, I am a robot. Regardless of how human-like Bran has made my brain, I am intelligent, and there are no gray areas. There will only be an affirmative or a negative response to any command I receive."

Sizx rolled her eyes and shook her head. She turned back to the control panel of her private capsule.

***

The control room in Tower Three got colder by the second, or maybe it was Ciaran's hands getting colder, Madeline thought. He couldn't perform the last search function on the computer, so he just dictated it to Jo. Jo was more than capable with computer systems, if not quite at Ciaran's caliber. She just typed in whatever he told her to—most of which sounded stranger than Eudaizian to Madeline.

The computer monitor flashed a signal. "Sizx has arrived at the gate in her private capsule," Jo said.

Ciaran stood up from a chair and approached the monitor. He glanced at the results and shook his head. "What we found is inconclusive. We still don't know who the traitor in our Eudaiz system could be or what the explosive command has to do with all this. Or with the number four or possibly the number three. I still can't think of anything concrete enough for us to act on."

Madeline said, "We'll just have to follow our plans. Ciaran, you go to the guest wing of Sciphil Three residence and get Gaia to help with the injury. Tadgh and Jo, you go to Tower Four to see if you can detect anything further. I'll go with Robert to Moira to ask for her advice."

Ciaran looked at her and smiled. She knew he liked her authoritative tone, especially when she bossed him around...for good reasons.

She continued, "I know we had a disagreement regarding Moira this morning. But we have to set that aside now. Solving this puzzle takes priority. But if I detect anything in Moira that leans toward your suspicion, I'll end the conversation with her. How does that sound, Ciaran?"

"Understood and agreed." He smiled again. If he had been at one hundred percent, that would have been his trademark, sinfully beautiful grin. Ciaran glanced to the corner and shouted, "Tadgh!" His brother disappeared right in front of their eyes.

"Oh my God, he's gone again!" Jo exclaimed,

Ciaran shook his head. "He just dematerialized, Jo. He'll be back soon." And he was right. In no time, Tadgh had rematerialized with a big grin on his face.

"Did you control it that time?" Ciaran asked.

"You could say—" Tadgh didn't have a chance to finish his sentence before Ciaran landed a punch on his face. "What the fuck?" Tadgh yelped.

"Grow up, Tadgh," Ciaran snarled. He strode out of the control chamber and headed toward the entrance.

Tadgh had given Ciaran a heart-stopping scare in Xiilok. But then, Tadgh couldn't control it because the ability had just been dumped on him. Now that he had managed to do it voluntarily, Ciaran's anger had just spilled over. Madeline had seen this happen many times. When it came to the safety of those he cared for, Ciaran felt vulnerable when he couldn't protect them. The fear he had suppressed when he thought Tadgh was dead must have been horrendous.

They exited Tower Three and saw Sizx's little capsule hovering next to Ciaran's. Sizx stepped outside and headed toward the group. Before she got to them, Ciaran said, "All of you get into my capsule and go to Sciphil Four residence. From there, Madeline, use a private capsule to get to where you need to be. Jo, you go back to Tower Four in a private capsule, too. Turn the trackers off so your capsules won't appear on the radar. Is that clear?"

Everyone nodded. Tadgh's eyes were angry, and he bit back profanity.

"Be careful," Ciaran said then glanced at Tadgh before he walked toward Sizx. Sizx gave everyone a courtesy nod. Then she wrapped Ciaran's arm around her shoulders and slid hers around his waist to support him as they walked toward her capsule.

Robert spun the little wheels under his feet and skated toward the group.

"Come on, she didn't need to help him. Ciaran can clearly walk by himself," Madeline muttered.

"I would hope she has a crush on Ciaran the size of a galaxy if I were you, Madeline," Tadgh said.

Madeline and Jo turned around and chorused, "What?"

CHAPTER 13

Sizz managed to park the capsule as close to the gate of the guest wing as possible. Because it was a private capsule, the security didn't clear it to park too close to the residential area of Sciphil Three. Even Ciaran couldn't clear it any further. If it was the official Sciphil capsule, they could have parked right at the front.

They left the cold connecting corridor and headed toward the guest wing. It was quite a walk. Ciaran felt his feet dragging. He didn't like being helped, but he might need it to even get to the door. Before he asked, Sizx slid her arm around his back and took some of his weight.

"Thank you," he said.

"It's my duty."

"When it comes to helping me, you always perform your duty in a private capsule?"

"The situation called for it. Based on—"

"It was just a poor joke on my part, Sizx. Don't worry—" Ciaran slumped to the floor, feeling the energy draining out of him in waves. *Trouble!* he thought. "I can't make it," he said.

"I'll call Gaia." She pulled out her communication device.

Ciaran grabbed her hand. "Don't. A call will leave a trace."

Sizx pulled him up. "Then you will have to walk." They staggered a bit but kept walking. Ciaran wasn't psychic, but he sensed a nasty presence in that corridor. The faint sound of rusty metal rubbing against rusty metal hovered in the air and echoed in his mind. Sizx showed no awareness of the sound. He tried to keep himself alert. Fatigue might lead to mistakes he couldn't afford.

***

Jo darted into her control room in Tower Four. She could see the damage to some of the computers. Although the explosion had been in her control room at the residence, because the system was interrelated, the explosion had fired the circuits in the motherboard. Tadgh followed Jo around, saying nothing.

Jo checked a keyboard and a monitor to make sure they were operational and had no undesirable effects. She dragged a chair over to prepare to run a full search. Tadgh flew over from behind, holding her up before her backside hit the chair.

"Come on, Tadgh, put me down," she snarled.

"You're not doing any work on these machines until I figure out what's going on."

"Then do it quickly. We're running out of time. Tell me. What are you thinking, Tadgh?"

"The number," he muttered.

"Like what, number four or three?"

Tadgh raised his hand and gestured for silence. "What happened when we discussed this out loud, Jo?"

"But I don't read minds."

He shook his head then walked around the room slowly.

"Yep, just ignore me," she muttered.

But Tadgh didn't seem to hear her anymore. He walked around the glass chamber that held her key stone—the key stone of Sciphil Four. He stood for a while, staring up at the stone. He walked around again. Then he grabbed a piece of paper and a pencil and sketched something. He crumpled up the paper and tried again.

She picked up a crumpled piece of paper. It was full of algebraic and geometric sketches—the kind that lived in her wildest nightmares. Her eyes crossed. Admittedly, she disliked modern algebra. But this was worse—it was like a weird, ancient algebra. She figured that algebra had originated way back in ancient Babylonian time, but she never connected that and her computer programs, let alone extraterrestrial or paranormal systems.

Tadgh stopped writing. He looked again at the key stone in the glass chamber then down to the floor. He measured with his footsteps. He walked around and around. Circled. Then he stomped his foot on a tile. He looked at her and grinned. He crouched and examined the edges of the square marble tile. He measured with his fingers. Then, at a spot that looked no different than the rest of the floor to Jo, he held down his thumb and then used his other thumb to press down on a corner of the tile.

The tile popped up from the ground and slid aside, revealing a hole underneath. An object shot up from that hole, flying at Tadgh's shoulder. But Tadgh didn't duck. In front of Jo's astonished eyes, he dematerialized his shoulder. The object flew past and hit the wall, shattering into a thousand pieces. Tadgh's shoulder returned to normal in a few seconds. He turned around and winked at Jo.

"That's impressive," she said.

"Thank you." Tadgh grinned and walked toward another corner of the room and repeated the process.

Jo figured he'd be unearthing four holes. But she knew he wouldn't want to discuss it out loud. She stood and waited patiently.

Tadgh lifted the fourth tile and muttered, "What the hell?" Jo charged over and looked. Unlike the other holes which looked like cable pipes, this one didn't have a hole. On the surface of the ground beneath the tile was the imprint of a black square. It looked as if a square object was meant to be inserted into it.

Tadgh looked at the keystone and saw a spark. They heard a cracking sound and felt the tower shudder. Freezing cold air whirled from the holes of the other three tiles, spinning around in the room. The key stone sparked again.

Waves of energy streamed out from Jo, lifting her off the ground. She felt like a magnet. The suction was incredible. Either she flew toward metal objects, or they flew at her.

Tadgh darted over, pulling her down and pinning her to the ground with his body on top. From underneath him, she could hear the metal cracking and clanking noises. Tadgh could dematerialize to avoid the hits. But he didn't. She guessed that the light objects would be flying first—computer frames, metal furniture parts, decorative items on the walls. They flew over to hit Tadgh and piled on top of him. For a moment, she thought the universe had collapsed on them. She heard Tadgh grunt he when was hit hard.

She had to do something about it. Getting him off of her wasn't an option when he was determined to stay on top. She wriggled, but couldn't get out. Then she remembered a decorative sword on the wall and thought it might become one of the flying objects. That's when she heard Tadgh grunt one last time and go quiet. His blood dripped down on her and pooled on the ground.

"Tadgh!"

There was no response. She tried to think. Magnet. Suction. Where had it all come from? It seemed as if there were no more small objects flying at them. But she could hear a stretching, wrenching noise as if the metal of the building was trying to detach itself from the concrete.

"Tadgh!" she called again. There was no response or movement from him.

CHAPTER 14

Ciaran fell to the ground at the entrance of the guest wing in Sciphil Three residence. He was totally out of it. "Gaia," Sizx shouted. From the hall, Gaia and her father, Liam, darted out immediately as if they had been waiting. Liam grabbed Ciaran's hand to check his pulse.

"No, he doesn't need you. He needs Gaia."

"I'm a medical doctor,"

"There's nothing medical about this. Get away." Sizx shoved Liam aside. "Gaia," she called. The little girl approached, as calm and composed as still water. She surprised Sizx.

"I'll see to him. Please leave the room," Gaia said.

***

Madeline and Robert stormed into the residence of Sciphil Six, Janei Chatel. She stopped them at the hallway. "I need to see Moira urgently," Madeline said.

"You said the same last time." Janei tossed her flaming red hair and cast a suspicious look at Robert, whose eyes were rolling with orange lights.

"Moira has just told me she isn't receiving any visitors now. She's busy."

"She'll make time for me. Let me past," Madeline growled.

Before Janei could object further, Moira's voice came from the corner of the room. "It's all right. I need to talk to her anyway."

Janei turned around. "You know how dangerous it is for you to come out that way?"

"I know. But there are things more important than my personal safety." Moira glanced at Madeline. "I'm glad Ciaran let you come here. I know he doesn't trust me."

Madeline narrowed her eyes. "What do you know?"

Moira smiled. "I know enough. I think you've seen evidence of that. I heard you're looking for a square."

Madeline shifted her stance.

Moira smiled again. "I have my sources. And I have part of the answer for you."

***

The sound of metal bending and cracking was getting louder. Soon, the tower would crumble on them. Jo willed herself to think harder for a way out. Between the gaps in the floor and the objects around her, she saw a reflection of light from the semi-transparent dome ceilings—the way in which the tower purified the best energy from the cosmos and sent it to the tower. And then she thought of something. It was her best shot at the moment.

She wriggled hard and managed to extract herself from under Tadgh's weight. As soon as she was out, she made a beeline for the main control panel. All the metal objects left Tadgh and flew through the air after her, including the sword that had stabbed Tadgh. She hated the sound of the sword as it left his flesh. But there was no time to think.

She ran fast. She flew at the dashboard and slammed her hand on a button. The eyelid screen on top of the dome ceiling shut immediately. As soon as that happened, all the metal objects stopped mid-flight and clanked to the floor.

Jo scrambled toward Tadgh, who was lying face down. The wound on his back was deep, but he was breathing, and she refused to believe it was lethal. She turned him over.

She shook his shoulders. "Open your eyes and look at me, Tadgh." His beautiful gray eyes opened slightly. He wanted to say something, but as soon as he opened his mouth, a stream of blood came out. "Oh, no. Please don't say anything." She wiped the blood away. "I'll take you to Tower Seven. Your chamber there will heal you. You're Sciphil Seven, for God's sake."

He closed his eyes. She shook his shoulders again. "No, no, you're not going to pass out. I can't carry all six foot two of you to Tower Seven. Not even a supernatural power would be able to do that. You'll have to stay awake and walk with me."

She tried to sit him up, but he said, "Give me a minute. Let me down."

"We don't have a minute."

"I can't make it to Tower Seven, Jo. I...only have a minute. Will you give me that?"

"I don't know what you're talking about. Let's go."

He closed his eyes.

"All right, all right. A minute it is. But please open your eyes." She didn't realize she was weeping.

"I hate to see you cry."

"Then get better."

"I'll try. But you...you have to promise me something..."

"What do you need, Tadgh?" Jo couldn't think. She couldn't imagine her universe without him. But she had to be strong. It was critical that she made no mistake here. He needed her.

"Will you marry me, knowing that you'll be a widow in only a minute?"

"What?"

He closed his eyes, and his voice was barely audible. "So...that's a no?"

"I'm not good news, Tadgh. We can be together. But I'm not good for marriage. Tadgh, come on...talk to me..." She shook his shoulders as tears streamed down her face. A minute was what he had given her, and she would make good use of that. "Okay, I promise. I'll marry you. But I don't want to be a widow. So I'll marry you only if you keep your promise and stay alive."

There was no response.

"Come on, if you want to marry me, then work harder. Pull yourself together."

Still no response. She wiped the stray hairs from his forehead and brushed the blood smears on his face away. "Open your eyes and look at me, Tadgh."

His eyes slowly opened.

"Good, you can hear me now. In Xiilok, you dematerialized and then put yourself back together again. Then at Tower Three, you dematerialized and went through nine layers of steel gates in a second. And just now, you dematerialized part of your body to avoid a hit and put it back in a nanosecond. You're the fastest learner in the cosmos, Tadgh. I know that sword must have punctured your major organs. Can you shift things in the wounded areas to temporarily heal the wound and get yourself back up? Then you can fix it later in Tower Seven."

His eyes blinked. It was working. Jo couldn't help but smile. "Come on, darling. Don't make me a widow too soon."

Tadgh closed his eyes again, but this time, she knew he was trying. His body temperature dropped considerably. She covered him as much as she could with her tiny frame when he shivered. In a few moments, his temperature was back to normal, and she could feel a strong, steady pulse and heartbeat.

"Stupid sword," Tadgh grumbled.

CHAPTER 15

Madeline opened her eyes to find Moira and Janei staring at her. She had tried three times to connect to Ciaran's mind without success. She could feel tears in her eyes and a lump forming in her throat.

"Is he down?" Moira asked.

"I suggest calling Ciaran's private communicator," Robert said.

"No private device is secure enough at the moment, Robert," Madeline said. "I have to go there in person."

"If my theory is correct, then you should be going to Tower Four," Moira said.

"I'm not sure your theory is correct, Moira. You're leaning toward Jo's prediction, which has to do with the succession line of Sciphil Fours. But Ciaran said the number three might play a part. And I can only be in one place at a time—"

The force that hit Madeline was incredible. Her body flew through the air and smashed into the far wall. She almost passed out. She stumbled to her feet as Moira and Janei darted in her direction.

A deep male voice boomed, "You are correct, Madeline. You can only be in one place at a time."

"Who are you?" Moira shouted, and then it was her turn to fly. Her body was lifted into the air and pinned to the wall. Janei darted toward her to help, but before she could get close, her body was scooped up and thrown against the far wall. She dropped down next to Madeline.

Robert's eyes continuously flashed red, green, and orange lights. He had been about to send out a rescue signal but was totally shut down before he could do so.

"There are four dematerialized forms of you against three women and a robot. Do you really feel that vulnerable?" Madeline said.

A deep laugh reverberated in the air. "You're very smart, Madeline. No wonder you're the First Councillor. I can certainly use you later."

Moira's body hovered in the air in standing position. It was as if she had been grabbed from behind and her mouth muffled. She wriggled hard but couldn't free herself from the captor.

The man's voice spoke again. "I have to take Moira with me. This woman never leaves the dimension in which she hides. Thank you for luring her out, Madeline. You and Janei must stay here until I sort out the other end."

Moira's body moved toward the entrance. Madeline felt herself being dragged and then incredibly cold hands pinned her down. She swiveled and kicked at the air in front of her, but it didn't help. She recalled what Ciaran had said about the fight he'd had with this dematerialized creature. When it had no material form, no ordinary weapon could get to it. Her kicks would have had no effect.

Ciaran had hit the creature with his mind blade. Perhaps she could do the same. She closed her eyes and mustered all the psychic ability she had to wield four swords. She slashed at the air in front of her and at whatever held Moira from behind. She couldn't see where the creature was that controlled Robert and Janei, so she slashed all around them.

She heard grunts and growls. She had hit it— or them.

Moira freed herself and darted toward the hallway leading to the basement chamber. That was the way to iilos, her hidden dimension. "Come with me!" she shouted as she ran. Janei dashed after her. Madeline was about to run, but then she saw Robert standing immobile. She ran over and turned him back on.

Moira and Janei had disappeared down the end of the corridor. Madeline charged after them. Whatever the creature had been, it didn't seem able to travel to Moira's dimension—her home for the last five hundred years. The creature grabbed Madeline again, and she brandished her mind sword again. She heard a clank and turned around. She felt her mind sword shatter, and her chest hurt.

Trouble! she thought. What had Ciaran said last time about this creature's weakness, assuming it was the same one? "Shine a light on the mirror, Robert!" she shouted.

Robert flashed his headlight onto a large mirror at the far end of the hall. The light reflected back, lighting everything in the hallway. In front of Madeline stood a sinfully handsome man. He had long, dark curly hair, striking eyes, and the face of a dark angel. There was something about him that was eerily attractive. He smiled at her.

"Hello there!" he said.

CHAPTER 16

Ciaran opened his eyes to see Gaia smiling at him. Liam, Gaia's father, sat on the sofa opposite them. He said, "I've checked your vitals, and they're all good." Ciaran nodded in appreciation and sat up. He could see that all the trees in the outside garden were dead again. Gaia had drawn contaminated energy from him before and replaced it with energy from the plantation in the garden. The poor trees and flowers hadn't had much time to regrow before she had taken their energy again.

"You will turn me into a vegetarian very soon, Gaia." Ciaran smiled at the eight-year-old Eudaizian girl. He still couldn't come to terms with the fact that Gaia was a conduit and could draw, convert, and transfer energy. She'd had this ability, and neither she nor her family had even known it.

Then it dawned on him that the woman Gaia had recently called "mother" was invisible—at least he used to think so. But now that he had seen what Tadgh could do, invisibility meant nothing. The woman must be in some form of dematerialization. He was sure of it.

Sizx raced into the main hall. "Are you okay? Do you need my reserved energy patch? You look very pale. Tell me what I can do."

He smiled. "Thanks, Sizx, but everything is under control now."

A text message from Tadgh came to his personal communicator. He activated the screen to view the message.

"What's that?" Sizx asked.

"He said there is a rabbit in my hat."

"But you don't wear a hat, and there are no rabbits in Eudaiz," Sizx said, confused.

"It's just Tadgh's way of saying he's okay, and I'm losing a bet."

"A bet?"

"Trust me, you don't want to know, Sizx. It's a guy's joke." As soon as Ciaran stood, he got a wave of sharp pain in his head. He grunted and slumped to the ground. Blood trickled from his nose. In a haze of pain, he heard Madeline's voice say, "Ciaran, the square is in the chapel." Her voice was cut off abruptly. He could hear her grunt as if she was in a fight.

His blood boiled. He needed to get to her. He needed to know what was going on at her end. *The chapel!* he thought. He looked up and saw Sizx's concerned face.

"You need to use my reserved energy patch. You've used it before," she said.

Gaia frowned. "You should save your energy, Ciaran. You only have ten percent , and you have to go back to Tower Three to recharge."

Now it was Ciaran's turn to frown, but he played along. He shook his head. "It's different this time, Sizx. I'm afraid that whatever caused my injury has contaminated my source of energy. I have to recharge at the source. But I'm not comfortable operating the Tower Three power chamber if I'm not one hundred percent clear about what caused the explosions."

"But your coronation is in a few days, and you can't last that long without recharging. Can your natural energy last that long?"

"No," Gaia said. "But there is another kind of pure energy you can get, Ciaran. It's in the chapel. You know that, right?"

"Gaia, the chapel is sacred," Liam scolded.

"But they're his ancestors. They'd give him the energy he needs."

The chapel was where all key stones of late Sciphils were worshiped. No one had access but the king Sciphil. Because Sciphil Threes had been the succession line of the king position, the chapel had been built beneath Sciphil Three's residence.

"All right. I'll go down there," Ciaran said.

"I'll wait here. I don't have access. If you need anything, just call me," Sizx said and sat on the sofa. Ciaran left the room and headed for the long hall leading toward the secluded area which connected to the chapel. Polished marble and stone columns flanked the pathway. He noticed there were no statues and no decorative items on the walls. He had never been down to the chapel—he'd never had a need.

He thought of Bran, the father he had known briefly. As a late king Sciphil, his key stone should be placed in the chapel. But he didn't even know where his father's soul had gone. Ayana had mentioned it once, and he now understood the pain in her eyes when she talked about it.

As for Ayana and Juliette, they had made sacrifices to build Silver Blood, and their essence would never be absorbed into any stone and placed in any chapel. They would become nothing. There was no materialized form that would hold their memories.

Wait, he thought. *Materialized form...* Materialized form that held memories of the death in Eudaiz—could it be more than a ritual? Could they be revived? Ciaran shook his head. He was probably overthinking this.

The imposing double door of the chapel stared at Ciaran. He shifted his left shoulder—a poor habit he had developed after that particular shoulder had suffered several injuries—and he placed his palm on the control panel. The computer verified him, and the doors swung open. As a mysterious light lit inside, and fog hovered on the ground and flowed out the doors, he heard a faint call from Gaia. Ciaran turned around and saw her charging down the hall, followed by her father and Sizx.

"Ciaran, watch out!" she yelled and threw fireballs in his direction.

CHAPTER 17

Madeline circled the man with daggers in her hands, looking him up and down. He smirked, but she knew it was only to disguise his anxiety. He was worried.

Only a minute ago, he had attempted to seduce her. Admittedly, he was attractive. And for a very strange reason, she felt drawn to him. But deep down, she knew the only man in this multiverse she loved was her husband.

She suddenly remembered Moira mentioning the reason she had waited in sorrow for five hundred years—it had started with a man who had a seductive power. A magician of the heart. A mastermind of delusion and confusion. Anyone with the ability to love could be his victim. The man in front of her might have something to do with that. Well, he had used tricks on her, so she would use tricks on him. That was only fair.

She psychically peeked into his mind. He hadn't expected that. For a brief moment, his guard was down, and she saw an illuminated square piece of stone in a chapel. She had no idea where the chapel was. But she knew the square stone she saw was what they had been looking for.

The man realized what she was doing and struck back at her. She quickly projected her psychic channel to Ciaran before the man materialized and attacked her. Her fencing skills were adequate, but unfortunately, his were outstanding. Plus, the daggers were not suitable for fencing.

He stood still, watching her circling him. She could tell he was planning something. He suddenly lunged at her, slashing at her right arm and causing her to drop her dagger. It clanked loudly on the floor then skidded away toward the other side of the room.

"Go away, Moira," she yelled and glanced behind him. He was distracted for a brief second. She took the opportunity to land a hard kick to his groin. Then she rushed down the hallway to the basement.

The kick in the groin seemed to slow him down because he chased after her more like a human than someone with special powers. And on a level playing field like that, she was faster. She turned the corner quickly and then jumped into the dimensional gate that would take her to Moira's dimension, but before she went through, she swiveled and landed another kick to the man's abdomen. He fell backward, skidding on the floor.

Then she moved through the gate. She guessed that dematerialized beings couldn't pass through to iilos. Only Moira knew the reason why because she was the one who had found that dimension. All Madeline cared about now was getting into a capsule and going back to help Ciaran.

"A capsule! How can I drive that stupid machine?" she thought and turned around, seeing that Robert had stormed into iilos after her on his little-wheeled feet.

***

At the end of the hallway in front of the chapel, Ciaran ducked aside when he saw Gaia's fireballs. Her fireballs weren't magic but were created from accumulated energy. They came with incredible heat and explosive power. She wasn't hurling them at Ciaran but at something several feet away from him. Ciaran realized Gaia must have seen something he didn't. He drew his daggers. Firing guns in here would be a bad idea. If it was the dematerialized creature he had fought before in Tower Two before Ayana died, no physical weapon would cause him any damage.

He looked at Gaia. If guns wouldn't work, neither would her fireballs. Ciaran darted in Gaia's direction. As he did so, something lifted her up and dragged her backward. Liam flew toward his daughter and tried to pull her away.

Ciaran remembered what had happened to Zach, but it was too late for him to do anything. The steel blade pierced Liam from the front to back of his chest. Gaia screamed. Liam dropped to the floor. Sizx charged over to pull Gaia from the creature. "Don't, Sizx!" Ciaran cried and darted over. He stabbed his dagger at the air next to Gaia, hoping to hit something. But it was just air.

Gaia started choking. Then Ciaran took a hard kick to his abdomen that sent him skidding backward.

"Let Gaia go, I'll give you what you want," he said.

There was a low growling noise, and then something said, "I want you dead!" A blast of freezing air lifted him off the ground and threw him against the far wall. Gaia fell to the ground. She scrambled toward her father's dead body, holding him and crying.

Ciaran could sense from the pressure of the air that a steel blade was heading his way. He made a quick mental calculation of the safe distance to leave between himself and Gaia and Sizx, and then he sent out a small mind blade. A loud clank echoed in the corridor. He immediately sent a second one in the same direction and heard a grunt.

Guessing that the dematerialized man had been injured, Ciaran jumped to his feet, grabbed Gaia, and ran quickly into the chapel. Sizx dashed after him. The cold breeze followed them. They heard a hard thudding noise, followed by the shattering of glass.

In the chapel, Ciaran turned around and saw the figure of a man slumped down right in front of the open doors to the chapel. The chapel doorway must have acted as a shield. The creature couldn't seem to get himself back up, and part of his body hadn't materialized properly and was transparent. Ciaran smiled, "I'm sorry for the inconvenience, but apparently all trespassers will be hurt. Do you think I should hang a sign at the door?"

There was a grumbling noise, and Ciaran assumed he was trying to say something, but it was incomprehensible. Then he passed out.

"How can you fight like that with only ten percent of your energy?" Sizx asked.

"Gaia discounted ninety percent when she said what she had given me. You wanted me to come down here, didn't you, Gaia?" He put her down and wiped the tears gleaming in her eyes. He pulled her tiny body into his arms. Her body shook with emotion. "I'm so sorry about your father, Gaia. I can't replace your family, but I'll do whatever it takes to make you feel at home." He wiped another tear that rolled down her face. She was very strong for an eight-year-old.

"Mother said you are to take the square stone and destroy it."

"Your mother was upstairs the whole time?"

"No. She came after you were back up. She said I have to send you down here to get the stone because the bad man was coming to get it."

Ciaran glanced at the unconscious man by the door.

"Will you kill him?" Sizx asked.

"I don't kill undefended men." He looked at Gaia. "He killed your father. Do you want revenge?"

Gaia shook her head. "It won't bring Father back to me. I am a conduit. Mother said I have to keep my energy pure. I cannot get blood on my hands. I am here to serve Eudaiz, and helping you is a part of the process."

Ciaran kissed her forehead. "You're an angel, Gaia. I wish to speak to your mother one day. Your parents would be very proud of you, wherever they are. Now, let's get the stone,"

Ciaran said and approached the compartment. The square black stone stared at him through the transparent shield. He verified at the control panel, and the door slid open. He picked it up. The stone was the size of his palm and was extremely cold to the touch. It was unusually heavy for a stone that size.

And then he felt a hard blow to the back of his head, and his world went dark.

CHAPTER 18

She was only a few inches away from the chapel door when she felt Ciaran's dagger slide around her from behind and press against her throat.

"You disappoint me, Sizx," he said. His voice was tinged with bitterness. She felt a pain in the part of her heart that could feel emotion.

"I didn't mean to hit you that hard."

"That physical blow didn't hurt as much as what you did. Gaia, are you okay?"

"Yes. She isn't as strong as she thinks she is," Gaia said as she stood up.

Sizx swallowed the lump in her throat. "You said you trusted me, yet you pretended you were injured?"

"No, I didn't pretend. I didn't find out until Tadgh told me I had a rabbit in my hat. He was referring to a human magic trick. And you're the only rabbit I could think of. You planned everything."

"No, not *everything*. My feelings for you are genuine. Twenty-five percent of me is human. When that part has feelings, I am not at fault." She could feel a tear rolling down her face. She could feel his body pressed against hers. She felt his heart skip a beat.

"You're not a natural Eudaizian?"

"No. I am fifty percent Eudaizian."

"And what is the other twenty-five percent of you? Who made you? Him?" Ciaran pointed to the man on the floor.

"I don't know who made me. But I know he saved my life."

The man on the floor started to move and wake up.

"Drop the stone," Ciaran said. She dropped it on the floor, and Gaia snatched it up.

"Kill me," she said.

"You think I won't?" Ciaran pressed the dagger harder, and a stream of blood ran down her neck.

The man in front of the door was now totally awake. He stood up and looked at her.

It was the first time in her life she had seen her Master in fully materialized form. He had attractive features, just like Ciaran. Dark hair. Striking blue eyes. The face of a dark, doomed angel. The fact that Ciaran was holding the dagger to her neck registered with him, and she saw genuine concern on his face. The words that came from his mouth were like music to her.

"Let her go," he said.

"Who are you?" Ciaran asked.

"My name is on the wall in that chapel. Let her go, and I will tell you what you want to know."

"Your name is in here, and your stone is in here. Aren't you supposed to be dead, Hoyt Flanagan?"

A smiled crossed his face. "A child conceived in the Red Stage of the Daimon Gate...you're way too smart. But I think your intelligence is more of a curse than a gift, Ciaran. Yes, I am Hoyt Flanagan, and I am the first Sciphil Four of Eudaiz. It took nine of us to build this universe the way you inherit it today. It shouldn't be the LeBlancs getting all the glory."

"There is no glory in what you have done."

"Maybe not. But my intention is to end the line of power to Sciphil Three and change it to Sciphil Four. I want to do it as peacefully as possible. I'm trying to minimize collateral damage here."

"You just killed a father right in front of his child. Is that what you call minimizing collateral damage?" Ciaran snarled.

Hoyt cleared his throat. "I don't think you're ready for the kingship, Ciaran. You're way too soft. Just like the first king, Pierre. It will get you killed."

"I might not be ready, but I am built for it. You have never been and will never be king regardless of how you maneuver your way through the multiverse."

Hoyt laughed. "You're too confident, Ciaran. I've gathered all the intelligence about you since the day you set foot in Eudaiz. Everything about you—your make, your biological and psychological profile. Whatever it is that the Daimon Gate has given you, I have that information. Remember how many times you used her reserved energy patch?"

Sizx wriggled, but Ciaran's arm around her was as hard as steel.

Hoyt continued, "Every single time you used it, your information was transferred to me. I know the way you think, the way you act. I might not be able to recreate a hundred percent of you, but I'm very close, I believe."

Sizx felt the tears streaming down her face now. She had been used. Was that what it took to be human? She was confused. Only twenty-five percent of her was human, but it hurt so much. It must be incredibly painful for Ciaran to feel her betrayal.

"Master..." she whispered.

"Sizx, I know you feel pain. But that's human nature. It will be better soon. I promise you," Hoyt said. He shifted his stance and tilted his head slightly to look at Gaia inside the chapel. Then he continued, "My plan is simple. On the day of your coronation, I will place the square stone in a secret place in Tower Four. When the power comes to you, it will be transferred automatically to Tower Four, and to me. I will be king. And you will be Sciphil Three, my Third Councillor. Everyone else will live in peace—except for the girl who is the current Sciphil Four. There can't be two Sciphil Fours at the same time."

"That's a very poor plan, Hoyt," Ciaran said.

"I respect you because you didn't kill me when I was down. I can easily replace you with the Ciaran I have created, but to thank you for your noble gesture, I will offer you a chance to serve as my councillor. You can stay there in that chapel for the rest of your life. But the minute you step out here and do not act like my friend, I'm afraid you will have to be one of the casualties..."

The sharp end of a dagger poked through Hoyt's chest, and he grunted with pain. Tadgh gradually materialized behind him. He pulled out the dagger and stabbed again.

Sizx's vision blurred with tears as she saw Hoyt's eyes glass over. He slumped to the ground.

"I told you it was a poor plan, Hoyt," Ciaran muttered.

Hoyt's body started to become transparent. The part around his heart started to melt. Sizx elbowed Ciaran and shoved him away. He lifted his hand as she did so to prevent his dagger from cutting her throat on his way down. She smiled at his gesture. He was a gentleman after all.

Her chest exploded, and she fell to the ground.

Madeline and Jo charged down the corridor. Madeline yelled to Tadgh, "Get away from him."

Tadgh dove aside as Hoyt's body exploded.

CHAPTER 19

From inside the chapel, Ciaran watched Tadgh scramble to his feet and try to leap into the chapel. As with Hoyt, he hit the shield at the door and landed on the ground with a thud.

"What the hell?" Tadgh growled.

"It seems the shield blocks anyone who has dematerialized, Tadgh," Ciaran said.

"She's going to explode! Get out of there, Ciaran!" Tadgh exclaimed, pointing to Sizx, who was lying on the floor.

Ciaran picked Gaia up and walked out. He handed Gaia to Madeline. "Liam was just killed," he told her. She gathered Gaia into her arms as the little girl teared up again.

Ciaran turned to go back inside the chapel, and Tadgh grabbed his elbow. "Hey, what do you think you're doing?" he asked his brother.

"She already exploded and will die soon. She helped us before, whether intentionally or not. How did you come to suspect her?" Ciaran asked.

"When she arrived to pick you up at Tower Three, I dematerialized to see if she was followed or if there was anything suspicious. I wanted to spook her, so I brushed her shoulder. It literally took her two seconds to jump. That only happens when she's expecting someone in dematerialized form to touch her. When she figured out that I might not be the person, she pretended to startle. I was about to tell you when you gave me a punch in the face."

"Well, I'm sorry about that."

"Apology accepted."

Jo approached. "Do you hear that clanking sound?" she asked.

"What?" Ciaran asked.

"It sounds like metal..."

"It's nothing," Tadgh said. "Did you say you wanted to go back into the chapel? I think Sizx is disappearing."

Ciaran nodded and turned on his heel to enter. Madeline gave Gaia to Jo and followed him.

***

Ciaran crouched next to Sizx. Sensing him, she opened her eyes. "I'm sorry, Ciaran."

"It's okay. You were used. You didn't know."

"Master saved my life. I owed him."

"I know. He planted a connector in your body, didn't he? So if he died, you would, too?"

Sizx smiled. "You know too many things, Ciaran. I'm sorry I didn't have a chance to learn more from you. But Master said there were twelve of us—the twelve seeds, he called us. I've never met the others."

"Now that he's dead, who will control the other eleven?"

"He didn't die. That was only a version of him," Madeline said.

"How do you know that?" Sizx asked.

"I just fought with four of them. When they combined into one, I gave him a very hard kick where most men don't care to be kicked. So if he had no trouble fighting you here, you were seeing different versions of him. He made fun of the fact we humans can be at only one place at a time. He's a magician, Sizx. And that means that whatever he's been showing you might be an illusion."

"Is being human that complicated?" Sizx asked.

"Yes, unfortunately," Madeline responded.

"I'm leaving, Ciaran." Her voice weakened.

"If you tell me how to fix you, I'll do it."

She smiled. "I don't know how. But thank you. Thank you for not killing me. That makes me think that having that twenty-five percent human is worth it..." She drew in heavy breaths. "Thank you...for never being harsh..." She shivered with the cold.

Ciaran gathered her into his arms.

"I know you're a man of your word. But I release you from your...promise... A part of me loves you, Ciaran..." she whispered into his ear. And then, she was gone. It was as if a piece of life had been taken from him. He wondered how many more of these sacrifices he would have to face on his way to power.

Maybe Hoyt was right—maybe he was too soft to be king.

He lay her down on the ground, and her hand pulled a button of his vest off then dropped it to the floor. He picked up the button and placed it in her palm. Her body glowed and then disintegrated, disappearing along with the button.

Madeline embraced him from behind. She stayed still and said nothing for a long moment. Then together, they went back outside and closed the chapel door.

CHAPTER 20

In the hallway, Tadgh grabbed the stone Gaia was holding and disappeared in the blink of an eye. Gaia gasped, "Wow, he was just as quick as Mother!"

Jo smiled at the little girl and put her down. "Is there anyone at all I can contact for you? I'm sure Ciaran would let them stay in the residence."

Gaia shook her head. "For security reasons, I'll stay in the residence by myself until after Ciaran's coronation."

"I don't think Ciaran will let you do that."

"I'm eight, you know."

"That's my point. You're too young to be by yourself."

"But I'm not by myself. I have Mother with me."

Ciaran approached. "She doesn't have a material form. She can't take care of you, Gaia. She can't even communicate with us without hurting our ears," he said.

"Where's Tadgh?" Madeline asked.

"Well, he appears to be out and about again—and this time with the stone. He thinks he's going to destroy it and scatter it across the cosmos like ashes," Jo said.

"Hoyt Flanagan will never return to his original form. He'll be lurking in the cosmos forever," Ciaran muttered.

"Was that worth it for the kingship?" Jo asked.

"I don't think he wants only the kingship. He wants to hold the controlling power over the cosmos," Ciaran said.

"So we're in this for the long haul," Jo muttered.

"I'm afraid so," Madeline said.

"What were you saying about Tadgh and the metal?" Ciaran asked Jo.

"I...he...I shouldn't say."

Ciaran held her shoulders and looked into her eyes. "Jo, please!" he said.

"We found the hole where Hoyt was going to place his stone. Tadgh destroyed the hole. And then there was an accident—he was stabbed from behind by a sword on the wall. He..." She teared up. "He thought he wouldn't make it to Tower Seven. So I asked him to shift things around the wounded area to heal it temporarily." She wiped a tear streaming down her face. "He fixed it. He healed the wound and stopped the bleeding... But the sword punctured his lung and cut into a corner of his heart. It left a metal residue. When he tried to heal the wound by materialization, the residue multiplied. Half of his lung and heart are now metal. He laughed and said now he has an iron heart and an iron lung, that he couldn't have asked for more. But I know he said that only because he knew he couldn't get rid of it." Then she broke down and cried.

Madeline gathered Jo into her arms. "Come on sweetheart. He meant it. It's a good thing. He might just become invincible."

"When he thought he was going to die, he asked me to marry him. I promised I would on the condition that he healed himself. After he figured out what had happened, he mentioned nothing about the proposal. If that metal heart is such a good thing, why did he pretend he never said anything to me about it?"

Jo turned to look at Ciaran. He had been unusually quiet. He stood still, listening to her with his hands in his pockets. She didn't know Ciaran as well as Madeline did, but to her, it looked like a sign of defeat. And if he didn't know what to do, who would?

Tadgh materialized at the end of the hallway and walked toward them with a grin on his face. "Hoyt Flanagan is gone. For good. I crushed his stone to dust and scattered it all over the cosmos. Good luck putting it back together." His smiled faded as he saw the look on everyone's faces.

Ciaran approached him. Tadgh stepped back. "Hey, brother, if you're going to punch me in the face, aim for the other side as my left cheek is still stinging from your last stunt. And for your information, I'm going to return this one twice as hard."

Ciaran said nothing but grabbed Tadgh by the collar and dragged him down the corridor.

"Hey, don't be a bully. Hey, stop that!" Tadgh protested before Ciaran pushed him into a side room and slammed the door shut.

"Is there going to be a scuffle in there?" Jo asked.

"If there's a fight, it's going to be more than a scuffle. But we're not going in. We'll wait here. Men need to do their things. And you wouldn't believe how stupid it's going to be."

***

In a small room just off the hallway, Tadgh shoved Ciaran's hands from his shirt. "What's wrong with you, Ciaran? Want a one on one? I'm ready. I'm not going easy on you this time." He shifted his shoulders and took a stance.

Ciaran looked at his brother, and then he started to laugh.

"What? What the heck?" Tadgh waved his arms in frustration.

"You scared the heck out of your woman."

"And you've never done so to Madeline?"

"Fair enough, my brother! Iron heart and iron lung." Ciaran shook his head and wiped a small tear that appeared in the corner of his eye because he was laughing so hard.

"It's not funny," Tadgh snarled.

"Yes, it is. It makes me think of those low-budget movies about medieval knights in poorly designed costumes. Okay, maybe it's not that funny if you're the one who has to deal with it. On Earth, the sugar in your blood could have killed you before you hit your teens. This metal issue is nothing. I'll have you fixed up by tomorrow."

"So why are we in here? I thought you were going to beat me up and then hug me and cry because I'm going to die tomorrow."

"What's the deal with you proposing to Jo and then pretending it never happened?"

"I thought I was going to turn into some kind of metal space creature. I didn't know what to make of it. It's nothing I can fix. I've got nothing to give her."

"I married Madeline in the Daimon Gate. I had nothing for her but blood and bruises. And here we are now with two kids, and she didn't even have a ring and a proper wedding."

"You can always wing it. I can't. Plus, Madeline is mad about you. I'm not so sure about Jo. She's not that into me."

"You're a disgrace to the LeBlancs, Tadgh. You should have seen her face when she thought you were going to die. That love is deep. You just have to be willing to dig for it. Jo is one of a kind, Tadgh. But you have to work for her. And as your brother, I'm going to help you do it."

Ciaran pulled a box out of his pocket and flicked it opened. Inside, two rings sparkled.

"Did you get these from the chapel?"

"No, you idiot. Zach got them for me when I sent him back to London to recruit Dan for Sciphil Five replacement."

"You're kidding me! The guy almost died on that mission."

"Not because of the rings! Will you accept this or not?"

Tadgh snatched the box from Ciaran and pulled out a ring with a small diamond and a delicate engraving of a very small red rose inside.

"That's Madeline's. Give it to me." Ciaran snatched back the ring. Tadgh looked at the one left in the box and saw an exquisite square black diamond sparkling at him. It was so...Jo. He was speechless.

"Thanks. I mean thank you very much. I would have never been able to wing this!"

Ciaran patted Tadgh's shoulder. "You don't have to wing anything. You love Jo, and you are my brother."

"So...we'll go out there. Is it going to be a double wedding?"

Ciaran shook his head. "Oh no, nothing is double. You go your way. I'll go mine. Plus, you and the two women we love smell disgusting."

"Hey, we were inside that thousand-year-old man's mouth. Try it for yourself and see how you smell."

"You need a shower." Ciaran grinned.

"Hmm...an opportunity for shower sex? You're getting more wicked by the second in this universe, brother."

Ciaran laughed. "I prefer to call it a wet proposal. Now you go and do your own thing. And I'll do mine. Just the way our precious women prefer it."

Tadgh and Ciaran pushed opened the door to find Madeline and Jo waiting outside. The dim light of the stars poured down through the sky dome and reflected on the polished floor, making the women they loved look irresistibly beautiful.

Madeline and Jo smiled at the brothers. And simultaneously, Ciaran and Tadgh clutched the rings in their pockets.

PART TWO

KING'S ENDGAME

CHAPTER 21

He was tall and strong for a nine-year-old kid, but Ciaran couldn't handle the sight of that cobra, reeling up from the ground, watching him, and hissing. He was afraid of snakes. And the way he normally handled that fear was by confronting it. To deal with his ophidiophobia, Ciaran had studied snakes—their habitat, their behavior, and how to kill them. He knew cobras shouldn't reside in the peaceful French countryside. Admittedly, it was a rather thick and mysterious bush that he had convinced his cousin George to explore—this was no meadow of sunflowers. But finding a cobra here should still be impossible.

"It's a cobra, George. Give me the shovel."

George was three years older than Ciaran and much taller. He jumped onto a large rock and reached his hand down for Ciaran. "I can see that. Jump up here. It won't climb."

"Give me the shovel," Ciaran snarled and held his stance on the ground. It was only a child-sized shovel they used to dig in the sand at the beach, and now George was using it to search for his rare mineral stones. But even a small shovel was much better than dealing with the snake bare-handed.

The snake slithered closer. Ciaran felt streams of sweat running down his back and his forehead.

"Get up here!" George shouted.

"No, give me the shovel!"

There was no way in hell he would run. It would haunt him for the rest of his life if he did—not the snake, but his cowardice.

"There! As you wish." George threw the small shovel to the ground and stayed up on the high rock. Ciaran picked it up just in time. The snake flew over, fangs bared with dripping venom.

It might have just been blind luck. Ciaran swung the shovel in a sweeping motion. He didn't know how it happened, but he realized the snake's head had dropped to the ground.

The body of the snake slithered forward. Or maybe it was convulsing before it died. He stared at those beady eyes of the severed head, and they looked right at him, the venom still dripping from those deadly fangs. It was a dangerous animal. It had attacked him, and he had killed it in self-defense.

Then everything was a blur. He heard George calling him, but he needed to get away from this. He dropped the shovel and ran. He might have run deeper into the bush. He didn't know. There were a lot of trees. He heard footsteps, but he didn't know who they belonged to.

He kept running.

When he reached the other edge of the woods, an area he had never been to before, he darted to a tree and was violently ill. There was no one around. He staggered to a large rock, climbed on top of it, curled into a ball, and drifted into sleep.

***

He didn't know how long he had been sleeping. Something cool and soothing touched his face. He opened his eyes and saw an angel. She smiled at him. Her touch was too real to be magical. He could feel the soft skin of her palm touching his forehead.

The scent of her was even more real—earthy like wildflowers.

"Bonjour," she greeted him in French and asked if he was fine. Her voice was light and gentle and had a melodic tone to it.

She helped him sit up. She smiled again and held out an opened lunch box.

"An apple!" His natural inclination made him say the word in English, but he understood her French well and could have carried on the conversation in French for hours.

"Oh, yes, it's my lunch. And it's an apple. You haven't seen one before?" She smiled and spoke in English. There was a twinkle in her eyes. He knew she was teasing him about his reaction to the apple.

At that point, he knew she wasn't an angel but the most beautiful earthly girl he had ever met. He looked down and saw he was still on the rock.

"You had a fever," she spoke again. "I was worried. But you're fine now."

"How long have you been here?" he asked.

"Since sunrise."

He looked up to the sky. It looked like late afternoon. But he had run from the snake at late afternoon. If she had been here since sunrise, that meant he had slept on this rock for at least one night. His father must have been worried sick.

He sat up and buried his head between his knees.

"Don't want to think about what's out there?" the girl asked.

He looked up at her. She was about thirteen. All he saw in her was beauty. It wasn't just her angelic look, but the purity in her eyes. She had just read his mind. He wanted to forget what was out there in the bush.

He was nine. But he had been receiving training in politics, philosophy, human ethics, science, warfare, and combat for as long as he could remember. The only explanation his father gave him for all the training was that he should be ready when the time came. As for what was coming, he had no idea.

Here, in this bush, Ciaran wanted only to be a kid. He wondered if he had run away from a snake—or something else.

"What's your name?" Ciaran asked.

"Lyla." She smiled again. "Would you like to hear some stories about magic?"

That was an experience Ciaran had never had. He didn't know much about fairytales. Mother had tried to read them to him, but she stopped because he was far too analytical about them. He couldn't just enjoy them as other kids did—like his brother, Tadgh, who just devoured the bedtime stories Mother read to him.

But Lyla's stories were different. They weren't merely fairy tales. They came from her heart. It was as if she had lived in the fairy land and was just relaying the information to him. There was nothing for him to analyze or judge.

Soon, he was lost in her stories.

Then the night came. She led him back to the edge of the woods and promised she would come back to the same spot to tell him more stories the next day. They met each other at the rock every day for a week.

***

It was the seventh morning, and he had come back to the woods to meet Lyla. The air was thicker. He knew something was wrong. He felt an emptiness in him that he couldn't explain. It was heavy. It was sad.

An old man stood next to the rock—no Lyla. The man turned toward Ciaran and asked with a thick French accent, "Are you Ciaran LeBlanc?"

He nodded.

"Follow me, please," the man said and turned on his heel.

CHAPTER 22

It was a cottage at the end of a small village. Like other French cottages, the house was small, charming, and inviting. But Ciaran's attention was sharply focused on Lyla, who was lying on the bed, looking as pale as a ghost. As he knelt next to her bed, she opened her eyes and looked at him.

"I am glad you could come. Sorry I couldn't make it to the woods today." She reached her hand out, and he held it.

His medical knowledge at this stage wasn't enough for him to do anything to help. But his gut instinct was telling him she was leaving him—forever.

"Lyla, tell me what you need."

She smiled. It was radiant on her tired face. "I'm afraid there's nothing you can do about this. I have terminal cancer, Ciaran. God will take me very soon."

"What kind of cancer? I'll take you to London. I'll tell my father. My family owns the largest pharmaceutical company on the planet. There is nothing my father can't do. Please let me tell him..." He knew he was just trying to bluff fate, and desperate tears rolled down his face.

"Your science can't hold back death, Ciaran. Do you believe in magic?"

"What?" He wasn't a believer, but he didn't have the heart to tell her that after spending six days with her in her fairyland.

"You didn't believe the stories I told you?"

"I did. I believe in magic," he lied.

She smiled. "I know magic. Not much, but enough to tell you this. I want to exchange the few days left of my life for the chance to save yours."

"I don't understand. But that doesn't sound good at all."

"My teacher lives in the woods. She's the one who teaches me magic. One of those spells will allow me to give my life force away to save someone I care for."

"I don't need it. Please don't do this."

"You didn't ask why it was you I wanted to give the rest of my time to. Most people would ask." She smiled again.

"I-I didn't know... Why me?"

"Because you will become very important. You will do a lot of great things. I want to be a part of that. A part of your journey, using whatever is left of me."

"How do you know all this?"

"My teacher. She shares many things with me. She said I would recognize the sign of giving when it came to me. And that sign was you. She couldn't save my earthly life. But she taught me how to live forever. Being a part of your journey is the way for me to do that. Will you accept my offer?"

"Please don't do this, Lyla." He started to cry. He had never cried so much in his short life.

"You didn't believe my fairy tales..." A tear ran down her face.

He panicked. "I do!"

"Then repeat after me..."

"Repeat what? No—" he began.

"I don't have much time left, Ciaran. Repeat after me."

"No! No!" he cried. He didn't believe in magic. He had lied to her. So why couldn't he lie to her now, just to make her happy? He repeated a strange word after her. Nothing was going to happen, he told himself. But if she died now, at least she wouldn't die resenting him for not believing in her fairytales and her magic.

He repeated the word three times as she asked.

There was silence.

Then in front of him was an explosion of white light. Lyla's body rose up and floated in the air. She opened her eyes, smiled at him, and dissolved like a fading angel.

Ciaran grabbed the edge of the bed. He felt his rage coming. It came at him so hard and so suddenly that his body vibrated. And then he heard the cobra hissing. It wasn't just one, though, but what looked like nests of them. Ciaran stepped outside the house and saw the village in chaos. At the far edge of the town, a river of snakes slithered in.

His rage was there, barely held inside his mind, and he was ready to savage. It had happened before when he was four. He had sent out his mind blade and dug up the entire hillside because wolves had killed his dog. He promised himself he would never do it again as he had no idea how many creatures he had unintentionally killed in that little forest he'd destroyed.

Now, he wanted to do it again and send these poisonous snakes into extinction. He wielded the blade in his mind, ready to storm the village.

Then he heard his father's voice. He felt his father's embrace and heard him whisper, "Calm down, Ciaran. Settle down, son."

"Father, the cobras are attacking the village. I have to kill them."

"Son, listen to me. I know you're angry. But you are hallucinating. The snakes are all in your mind."

"But I saw the cobra in the woods, Father. Ask George."

"Yes, that one was real. But the ones you're seeing now aren't. If you send out your mind blade based solely on unjustifiable sentiment, you will kill innocent people."

"I don't want to justify anything to anyone, Father!" Ciaran shouted and charged out of the house.

CHAPTER 23

She kissed him. Perhaps that was the gentlest way Madeline could wake her husband and shake him loose from whatever was on his mind. She had been watching him as he slept. She tried to peek into his mind, but it wasn't possible when he was sleeping. Her theory was that when he was asleep, his mind was not in an active state, so she couldn't look into it. He must be having a nightmare. She hoped it was a nightmare because a nightmare was simply a dream. But if it was a flashback disturbing him, it reflected past events—and those she couldn't fix.

"Good morning, First Councillor. How long have you been up?" He opened his beautiful gray eyes and looked at her.

"Since sunrise."

He laughed. They didn't have a sunrise in Eudaiz because they didn't have the same solar system as Earth. He held her hand and kissed the finger with the ring he had put on it the day before.

"I'm still liking it," she said and smiled.

He frowned. "Does that mean there's a chance you will grow tired of it? How soon?"

"I'd like to have at least an anniversary to see what it's like. When you have a moment to convert Eudaizian time to Earth time so I have some sensible time bearings, then we'll talk about it. But it won't be soon."

He smiled at her.

She continued, "It's your big coronation day today..."

He rubbed his thumb on the dimple on her left cheek and pulled her down to lie on the bed beside him. "Yes, it is—in Eudaizian time," he said and kissed her.

She responded to his kiss. Their bodies fit together so well. She knew he always craved her soft skin touching his, so she pulled her sleeping gown off. A soft purr of pleasure erupted from deep in his throat when her hands roamed his body. He responded to her touch with the same passion she had given him.

They moved together in rhythm—every movement of their bodies, every stroke of their hands, every breath. Nothing was out of sync. Their lovemaking was a harmonious piece of music. Only their passion for each other existed.

For a while, Madeline remained curled into his arms. She wanted to stay there as long as possible. She didn't look forward to the day stretching ahead of them. Part of her wanted this coronation day over and done with. Part of her didn't want to deal with it at all.

He pressed a kiss on her temple. "Thank you," he said.

"You don't have to thank me for sex. We're married after all," she said, turning to lie on her back and examining the stunning red stone on her ring.

"You know that's not what I meant. You want me to settle and be ready for the day. So thank you. Again." He sat up.

"What's on your mind, Ciaran?"

"Now?"

She sat up and looked into his eyes. "Yes, now."

"I think the ring looks just like you. Exquisite." He held her hand again and kissed it.

Damn. She'd tried, but she couldn't read his mind now, even when he was awake. Had he developed a defense mechanism against mind probing? She saw the word *Lyla* as he woke, and then her channel went blank, and she could see nothing else. She'd have to work Lyla into a question somehow as naturally as possible.

Ciaran hopped off the bed, heading toward the bathroom.

"I hope the ring is expensive. It's not like you would ever buy anything cheap..." she muttered.

He stopped and turned around. "You're priceless to me, Madeline. Nothing could ever compare to what we have together. Our relationship. Our family. But if you must know, it's a red diamond, and it's worth about two million dollars per carat on Earth."

"What?" Madeline exclaimed.

"Lucky for us, we don't need money in Eudaiz." He grinned. Turning, he headed again to the bathroom.

Now she sounded like a gold digger. *Damn it.* She had wanted to ask him about Lyla. But before she could muster another strategy, Robert stormed into the room. The lights on his forehead flashed a continuous strobe of red and orange.

"Robert, what did we say about knocking?" she snapped.

"I did knock."

She looked at the door panel. The green light there suggested it had flashed four times.

"What's with the orange lights?"

"I came to give you the status report for the coronation. I input the report into the bedchamber screen so you can watch from here. But you have to turn on the screen."

"All right. I'll do that. Is everything okay?"

"Yes. One hundred percent. The council meeting has been arranged. Sciphil Eight is back at his station and will be at the meeting."

"So I'm asking again—what's up with the orange lights?"

"Your dress code for the coronation is rather inappropriate."

Madeline cursed to herself. She hadn't put her clothes back on. She snatched the gown from the floor where it had dropped and scrambled back into it. "All right. Now I can look at the report," she said. Then she looked at Robert and said, "You're a robot. Aren't you supposed to be neutral about dress code?"

"I am a learning machine. I have learned human fashion tastes and preferences from you and Ciaran."

"Well, here's something new for you to learn. That was a rhetorical question, and it didn't require an answer. Now if you could leave me alone to read the report, it would be greatly appreciated."

"Affirmative. There is a piece of information I think I should report to you, not to Ciaran."

Her head jerked up. Robert only said that when there was something he detected that would go against Ciaran's best interest, and if he were to act on his free will, he would act against himself.

"What? Tell me. Hurry!" she said and glanced at the bathroom door.

CHAPTER 24

Pete Chandler had been Sciphil Nine for more than thirty years, Earth time. He joined the council of Eudaiz late in life and had thus maintained a strong connection to Earth. Regardless how much time passed, he didn't think the transition had changed him. He thought like a human, and he still acted in humankind's best interest. His council friends had died off in such a short time. Getting rid of Kyle Wolf had been the only good thing to happen during such hard times. But as far as he was concerned, the danger ahead was greater than ever.

Hoyt Flanagan was a five-hundred-year-old devil whose life's mission was to take over Eudaiz and destroy the LeBlancs. He had five hundred years' worth of experience, knowledge, and skills that had created a hybrid of magic and science—an asset nourished by the vicious flame of hatred.

"Sciphil Five, Dan Chandler, has arrived at the residence," a robotic voice announced.

"Let him in."

Dan was his distant nephew. He had recommended him for this position because of his natural connection with and understanding of the supernatural. Ciaran had extensive knowledge about all subjects, but his knowledge came from research. Dan understood the supernatural as if it had been a part of him since he was a kid.

"Something is wrong," Dan said as soon as he entered the grand hall of Sciphil Nine's residence.

"Well, you need to be a bit more precise than that, Dan."

"Something feels wrong."

"Dan, I know your appointment was rushed, and you didn't have enough training. But you're in charge of a district of sixty billion citizens. You must give your staff better directive orders."

"It's not about District Five, Pete. It's about the coronation."

"Let's not waste time. The coronation will be on in a few units." Pete frowned. "I know we lost Sizx, and every connection she established in the system will have to be rebuilt. And I know Hoyt Flanagan has been plotting to take over for centuries, but Tadgh has already destroyed his key stone. There's no way he could get back into his form to usurp any power in Eudaiz. And we still have to be careful about everything else because I know Black Rock and Xiilok are gathering their hired soldiers. But the Daimon Gate has secured all entrances to Eudaiz. Even if they can slip soldiers in through wormholes, they can't come in large numbers. So what else do you know that I haven't mentioned?"

"Cobra."

"What?"

"It's a snake—"

"I know what a cobra is," Pete cut him off. "What does a cobra have to do with the coronation?"

"I've been seeing the image of a cobra in the last few days. The cobra has many mythical meanings, and one of them has to do with the first Egyptian pharaoh."

"I'm afraid I know nothing about Egyptian mythology. You could talk to Ciaran about it, but you'd better have something more substantial than the fact you saw a snake in your dreams. He spoke highly of the way you bluffed Kyle out of killing Juliette, especially given you had no idea what Silver Blood was."

"I'd prefer to discuss this with Ciaran in private. But the council meeting will start soon. And my communication channel couldn't get through to Ciaran for some strange reason."

Pete sighed. "They're rebuilding all communication channels right now. You know what happened with Sizx. She was the mole Hoyt placed in our system. She was the head of intelligence, and we can't risk any contamination in the communication channel while the coronation is going on. We have to rebuild everything."

"Do you think Sizx was the only mole?"

"Ciaran wondered the same thing. But we don't have time for further investigation. Ciaran said we'll just have to play it by ear. It's good you can't use the system to communicate. I don't know who we can trust."

Dan sighed. "What about the new intelligence head? I understand that Ciaran can't trust anyone at the moment. But how can you operate if you trust no one?"

Pete shook his head. "I don't know. I guess his experience managing his conglomerate on Earth comes in handy. If you need to talk to Ciaran, it's best to go to his residence."

"You think I haven't tried?"

"You mean your capsule network is down, too?"

"It kept rejecting my commands."

"Okay, let's just go to the council meeting. We'll try to talk to Ciaran there." Dan nodded. They turned and exited the grand hall. Pete continued, "So you saw a cobra in your dreams... Anything else?"

Dan shook his head, "The cobra is bad enough. It's not just a cobra, it's a legendary one. I can tell. It's the cobra that bit Re—the king, the god of all things, the first pharaoh. Legend says the cobra was created by Re's daughter Isis because she wanted him out of power."

Pete raised an eyebrow. "Do you realize you're talking about a legend? That means it might be pure superstition."

"Yes, but Hoyt was a sorcerer, wasn't he? Ciaran said Hoyt was the one who placed the ennead codes to cause trouble with other Sciphil officiations. Hoyt must know all about Re and the legendary cobra."

"Lucky for us, he's dead!" Pete muttered as a private capsule approached.

"Are you sure about that? Madeline said there were multiple versions of Hoyt."

"He can dematerialize and create multiple versions of himself, but they are only copies. Each individual has one core energy. In the language of superstition, that means one soul, and in Eudaizian, it means one essence represented in a key stone. Tadgh destroyed Hoyt's key stone and scattered the pieces across the cosmos. He can no longer have a materialized form. Therefore, he can't be king of any universe. So what are you saying? He's going to turn into a snake?"

"I'm serious, Uncle!"

"I can tell that. But to convince Ciaran, you may need more than a snake in a dream."

Dan shrugged, put his head down, and approached the opened door of the capsule.

CHAPTER 25

The semitransparent ceiling of the hallway leading to the grand meeting hall let in a spray of bright white light. It was the equivalent of morning on Earth. Ciaran glanced at his wrist unit. It stated unit sixty-seven in the morning, Eudaizian time. He was early to the meeting. He made a mental note to ask Tadgh to develop a system to convert the universe's time to a more Earth-friendly time reference.

When he had finished in the bathroom earlier, Madeline was no longer in the bedchamber. She had left a note on the table. "See you at the council meeting. Love. Madeline."

Everything about that message was wrong. The tone. The writing. The signature. He didn't like it one bit. He approached the control panel in the bedchamber to call her then decided against it. That would defeat the purpose of her handwritten note. She didn't want it in the system. She would psychically channel into his mind if she wanted to bypass the system. She'd done it before. But there had to be a reason she hadn't done it already.

The heavy double steel door slid open in front of him, revealing a round room with round meeting booths located around a central platform. The individual booths housed the eight Sciphils. His booth was at the center of the platform. Unnecessarily grand, Ciaran thought. He would reorganize this into a corporate-style meeting room later.

He didn't see Madeline in the meeting room. Tadgh and Jo arrived just after him. Pete, Dan, Zach, and Janei were already in their booths. And there was a new face—Aiden Felix, Sciphil Eight— who gave Ciaran a dismissive look as he came in. Silence. There was no conversation. Zach and Dan were eyeing Aiden, who remained seated while everyone else stood when Ciaran entered the room.

He nodded to acknowledge everyone and then seated himself. "Thank you for being here. Madeline will be here soon," he said.

"She must be playing the husband-wife privilege game. As the First Councillor, being late is sloppy. She should be disciplined," Aiden said. He had a thick South African accent. He stretched his long, lean body out, leaned back in his chair, and waited for Ciaran's response.

"Dickhead," Tadgh muttered.

"Oh, is that a new code of conduct for new councillors—using profanity in place of respectful English? What kind of education do you have, Sciphil Seven?" Aiden asked.

Ciaran smiled and spoke before Tadgh responded. "I don't believe we've been properly introduced. In fact, I don't recall seeing your name on the council list when we officiated new Sciphils."

"I was on a mission," Aiden snarled back.

Ciaran frowned. "You are a very experienced councillor, Sciphil Nine. So please correct me if

I'm wrong. Important missions must be passed by the council and reported on the log. Otherwise, it's considered private matter—meaning *not* important."

"That's correct, Ciaran," Pete said.

Ciaran smiled. "Sciphil Eight, because you were tending to private matters and missed the previous officiations when we needed the help of experienced Sciphils, I can't trust you to be part of the coronation today."

"You've got to be kidding."

"I am not in the mood to joke on my coronation day." Ciaran looked at Aiden, whose face reddening.

"You need me! You need all eight Sciphils in their towers to connect the power for your coronation."

Ciaran arched an eyebrow and leaned back in his chair. "That would be the ideal scenario if all Sciphils cooperated and acted in the best interest of the coronation. You weren't here for us when we needed you. How can I be sure you will be there when we need you during the coronation?"

"I would—"

"I haven't finished, Sciphil Eight! Connecting the power during coronation gives Sciphils privileges and access to the power and the Silver Blood down the track. You don't want to miss out. That is why you are here."

"Being a Sciphil gives me privileges. Don't tell me you accepted this position out of the goodness of your heart."

Ciaran stared at Aiden for a short moment then said, "I don't need people like you in the council. You're dismissed."

"You can't dismiss me. You aren't king yet!" Aiden stood up. His face was crimson, and he looked ready to charge at Ciaran.

"I am in the king Sciphil position. I have a good counseling team, and I can't see that you have any part in it. So I repeat, you're dismissed."

"You'll regret this!" Aiden yelled as he turned to leave.

"You are not free to leave," Ciaran said. "Guards, detain Sciphil Eight."

"Don't you dare!"

"I'll release you when the coronation is completed. I don't need another issue to deal with. We have spies in high places in Eudaiz." As the guards pulled Aiden out, Ciaran went to the control panel. "I will set Tower Eight on auto operational mode." He turned on the communication channel to call the new head of intelligence.

A young Eudaizian with glowing golden skin and sandy hair appeared on the screen. "Yes, sir."

"What's your name?"

"Jakerandrum Hyth Sidg Sammdrie."

Ciaran raised an eyebrow.

"But people call me Jake, sir."

"All right, Jake, how long can a tower run on auto operational mode?"

"One unit, sir."

"Good. That's all I need from you,"

"Which tower would you like to set run on auto operation, sir?"

"Call me Ciaran."

"Yes, sir... Ciaran."

"I'll take care of the auto operational mode, Jake. That's all for now."

Jake nodded and vanished from the screen.

"You can't function efficiently without trusting people, Ciaran," Sciphil Six, Janei Chatel said.

"I'd prefer inefficiency to collapsed operations. Trusting the wrong people today could kill any operation and cause catastrophic consequences for Eudaiz. I apologize if I offended you, Sciphil Six."

Janei smiled. She was more than a hundred years old, but she looked to be in her fifties. Her skin was a shimmering golden shade, and her face glowed.

"All Sciphils have their talent. I'm sure that's how you were appointed in the first place. What is your unique skill, Sciphil Six?" Ciaran asked.

She smiled again. "All you need to know is that I do have talent. And I will contribute when it is in the best interest of Eudaiz. As for what my talent is, I can only tell those I trust."

Ciaran grinned. "Very well, Janei. We shall leave this matter alone for the moment."

"Ciaran, I need to talk to you in private," Dan said.

As Ciaran turned to go outside the room with Dan, the computer screen flashed a message: "Intruder alert!"

CHAPTER 26

Madeline stormed into Sciphil Six's basement after her robot, Robert, had helped her break the locking code. The basement was the only gateway to Moira's hidden dimension. She hurried down the hallway but slowed a bit for Robert, who was spinning the little wheels under his feet as hard as he could but still fell behind.

She didn't know what Robert had done, but the system recognized that she had an invitation to Sciphil Six residence. She moved past the entrance and through the doors effortlessly. "You've done an amazing job in creating this fake invitation, Robert. You'll get a promotion after this."

"Is a promotion a form of career advancement? That is what my dictionary says."

"Yes, Robert. Just tell me what you want, and I'll ask Ciaran to give it to you."

"I'd like to take a trip to Earth. I'd like to learn more about the human species."

"Well, your first lesson is not to call them species when you speak to them. They won't like that."

"I will record that human communication etiquette."

Madeline raced along the duplication of the Irish countryside toward Moira's house. She had traveled this route a few times by now, but this time, it seemed to take decades.

Earlier, Robert had retrieved a recorded message from his spy device. It didn't make sense to him, but he calculated a high probability of the significance of the event and thought it to be something of interest to Madeline and Ciaran because their previous trip to Moira's had created a disagreement between them. Subsequently,

Robert used the technology Bran had created and Ciaran didn't have access to. He analyzed the situation and reported to Madeline.

In the message, Moira muttered things that might have seemed nonsense to everyone else. But to Madeline, it sounded like her children might be coming out of the boxes early. Moira wasn't pleased at all about her miscalculation. Only mothers had these kinds of instincts, Madeline thought.

"Hell, technology!" Madeline as she stood in front of Moira's grand hall, finding it empty and cold. "Moira!" she called out.

There was no response.

"Moira, I need to speak to you!" she called again.

"All right, all right," Moira grumbled as a side door slid open. Her attention was focused on a portable device.

"I trusted you with our children's lives, Moira," Madeline said. "Today is Ciaran's coronation. Could you have chosen a worse day on which to have a technical glitch?"

"There's no problem with my technology."

"We heard you talking about your miscalculation."

"You heard me? How?"

"It doesn't matter now. We just know."

"There's nothing wrong with my technology, but do you know how difficult it is to convert inter-universal time? Don't worry—your children will come out as expected. They'll be perfectly healthy. But I gave you the wrong time."

Madeline narrowed her eyes. "I don't believe you."

"Up to you. But we do have a real problem regarding the timing. Because children conceived during the Red Stage of the Daimon Gate are special, they suck up a large amount of the universe's energy when they come out."

"How much? Enough to kill people?"

"No, but enough to draw attention from a very long distance away in the cosmos, especially from those who have a vested interest in them."

Madeline felt a cold sweat break out along her spine. There were many people who had vested interest in their children, primarily their enemies—and they hadn't yet identified them all.

She knew she and Ciaran disagreed on certain things regarding the children and Moira, but she didn't think she could make this decision or solve this problem on her own. Not today. Maybe not even on her best day.

"I can bring my super-soldiers into the Daimon Gate and guard their chamber when they come out," Moira offered.

"I don't like the implications of taking an army into the Daimon Gate," Madeline said as her level of panic rose.

"It's not a large army. But even if I do take my soldiers, it still might not be enough when we encounter strong enemies. And my soldiers are still not able to handle Xiilok fighters."

"What if the children are the decoys, and the real attack will be on Ciaran?" She couldn't afford to make a mistake today. "I have to call him," she said.

"Are you sure? From here? Using the system?" Robert asked.

"What choice do I have?"

"You can channel into his mind. You've done that before," Robert suggested.

"My ability isn't stable. It's not a switch I can turn on and off when I want. Plus, Ciaran isn't a psychic. I couldn't look into his mind this morning. The stress of today's event had probably raised all of his psychological defense mechanisms. I can't hook into his mind right now."

CHAPTER 27

Ciaran rushed toward the control panel. The computer was still flashing an alarm, and he could see a red target on the screen. The monitor showed the target moving along the corridor from the outside.

Jake came on the screen. "We have identified a target traveling outside the protected corridor. There's no breathable air in that area, so we assume it's a creature of some kind. It's small in size but creates an incredible suction of energy wherever it goes. We have a visual—should we destroy it, sir?"

"Show me," Ciaran said.

What they showed him wasn't exactly visual. His quick evaluation of the blurry image led him to the conclusion that surveillance cameras were poorly equipped in nonhuman arenas. That was a critical mistake he would have to fix later. The monitor revealed the shadow of a small creature with a human shape. Ciaran glanced at the image and said, "Don't shoot. I know who it is." He turned to go outside.

"Are you certain, sir?" Jake asked in a panic.

But Ciaran had already exited the room.

***

Running along the corridor, Ciaran located a hole in the wall. He backed away from it. The air outside was thin, and the suction from the outside was incredible. He remembered vividly when Madeline had been flung outside one of those holes. She had nearly died.

He charged toward the station and jumped into a hovering rail-free capsule. As he navigated back to the broken corridor, he hovered the capsule. Through thick layers of cloudy air, he could see a small shadow below. He landed and put the capsule in self-protective mode just in case things went wrong. He glanced outside, tucked and secured his daggers, then opened the door.

He could see the small shadow a few feet away. He approached with caution. As he got closer, he could see it was the person he had expected.

"Gaia," he called out, shaking the shoulders of the girl lying on the ground. Her teeth chattered, and she barely breathed. "Hang in there, sweetheart. I'll take you inside." He held the girl in his arms and darted back toward the capsule.

Once inside, he sat Gaia down on a chair and increased the temperature.

"Thank you," a woman's voice rang out, and a sharp pain shot through his head, sending him to the floor. Every cell in his body vibrated with the frequency of the voice.

"Fuck me!" Ciaran snarled. "Can you please wait until I finish defrosting the girl?"

Soon, Gaia warmed up, and her skin regained some of its pink color. Ciaran turned on the light in the back compartment and took Gaia there. "Can you absorb some energy from that?"

As a conduit, Gaia would be able to draw energy from various objects for her supply. She would be self-sufficient very soon. But at the moment, she was too weak. He helped her raise her hand. When her arm was firmly in place, he released her hand. He had known instantly that the small shadow was her. As far as he knew, in this universe, she was the only conduit in the central Sciphil zone.

Gaia kept her hand palm up, fingers toward the light. The light flickered and went off. Ciaran could see a light current streaming into Gaia via her fingertips.

She smiled gently and looked at him.

"That's enough for now. I'll take you back to central. There you can draw energy as much as you like."

She nodded as he carried her back to the chair.

"My mother said thank you. She knows you took a risk to come and rescue me."

Ciaran realized that the woman who called herself Gaia's mother could communicate with him via Gaia. He didn't trust that woman. He didn't believe she was Gaia's mother. As to who she was and what her motive might be, he made a mental note to find out after his coronation.

"Gaia, I'm quite busy today. We'll talk tomorrow. I need to know why you ran to central, who your mother is, and what she wants from us. But for now, we have to get back to central before people start to panic."

He turned to go to the control panel to start the capsule when he heard Gaia's small voice.

"Mother told me to go to central to help you. I tried to draw energy on the way, but I accidentally punched a hole in the wall. Then, when I was sucked outside, I couldn't get back in. The suction was too strong for me. There was no air to breathe and nothing out there for me to draw energy from."

Ciaran spoke into the air. "You asked your daughter to go to central by herself? You know how dangerous that is. What kind of mother are you?"

"You need help," Gaia said.

Ciaran crouched next to the chair. "I assume you're speaking on behalf of your mother. Look,

Gaia, I know you've just lost your father. You're lonely, and you need parental care. But a true parent would never risk harm to their child. Whatever this woman has been telling you, can you promise me you won't follow?"

"But I want to help you."

"You see, this woman asked you to go to central, and you almost died. You're too young to participate in any battles. I appreciate your wanting to help, but I don't want you near the towers during my coronation. Do you understand?"

Gaia nodded.

"Good girl." As Ciaran stood to return to the control panel, Gaia tilted her head and looked off into space for a moment, and then she spoke again.

"You will be attacked today. Your power will be diverted, and you will be ambushed. It will be catastrophic."

Ciaran turned to look at Gaia. "How do you know, Gaia's mother? What's your name?"

The voice that came out of Gaia's mouth now was no longer a child's voice. The little girl's eyes had gone distant and glassy. "I have no name. I have no body. But I do have my mind."

"Well, don't use that mind to control a child's!"

"She is my daughter."

"Liar! What do you want?" Ciaran snarled.

"I am your friend."

"Then prove it, goddamnit. Prove to me that there is a stranger in this universe I can trust. Make fairytales become reality!"

"You don't have to trust me, but we have the same enemy."

Ciaran chuckled bitterly. "I have more enemies than I have friends. Which one do I share with you?"

"Hoyt Flanagan." The woman's voice was calm and throaty. Ciaran didn't have psychic ability, but he felt an odd connection to the woman—and he didn't care for it. His gut told him that if this woman had a tangible form, she would look like someone he knew very well.

CHAPTER 28

Ciaran strode into central holding Gaia in his arms. She could walk, but she was still too weak to move fast. He turned into a smaller hallway and spoke as he walked. "How do you want Gaia to help me?"

The woman's voice came out of Gaia's mouth again. "I think that during your coronation, Hoyt will attack you from multiple directions. You will have to use a large amount of energy to fight him—an amount you don't have. So Gaia will help you draw energy from other sources."

"How will Hoyt be attacking me?"

"I don't know, and we won't know until he actually does it."

Ciaran slammed his palm on a verificator, and a small door opened. Behind the door was a small lab. He strode in and put Gaia on a bench. He tucked a sheet around her and adjusted the room temperature.

"She doesn't need to be tucked in."

"I know Hoyt will try with every breath he has left to jeopardize my coronation. This universe is at war, and I will do my best to save as many as I can. But I will not send a child to battle." He slapped a medical patch on Gaia's arm to sedate her. Then he turned on his heel and left the room.

***

Dan raced over when Ciaran entered the meeting room again. "I need to speak to you urgently."

"Go ahead."

"If Madeline doesn't get here quickly, she'll be late and have to go straight to her tower, Ciaran," Pete said.

"Understood," Ciaran muttered.

"Do you need me to find her?" Tadgh asked.

Ciaran shook his head. Before he could say anything, a call from Madeline flashed on his wrist unit.

Jo glanced at the screen. "It might not be her," she said.

Ciaran glanced at the screen and nodded. "It's her. And she's desperate." He picked up the call. Madeline's face appeared on the screen instantly. He took one look at her eyes and saw trouble.

"I'm in iilos with Moira. I know we disagree about this, but Moira says our children will come out today. She miscalculated the timing."

"She did that on purpose," Ciaran growled. "What does she want now?"

"She said when the children come out, they will cause a disturbance and draw energy sources. They'll catch the attention of anyone with a vested interest in them."

"Our enemies," Ciaran said.

"That accounts for more than half a multiverse," Sciphil Six, Janei Chatel commented.

Ciaran realized he had engaged the conversation with Madeline in the meeting room, and all available councillors had heard him. He glanced around the room. But it was too late to back out, so he continued, "How does Moira suggest solving the problem *she* created?"

"She said she could take her soldiers into the Daimon Gate to protect the children."

"Right. She wants me to allow the gate to open so her army can come in. Then from the Daimon Gate, her men could easily head to Eudaiz or any of the participating universes. It's very clever, but it won't work with me. I assume you've handled Moira?" Ciaran said.

Madeline smiled and tilted her wrist unit toward the corner of the room to show Ciaran that Moira was tied up to a chair.

Ciaran smiled. "We need you back here right away, Madeline."

"What about the children?"

"I'll sort that out—" Ciaran grunted in pain and put his hands to his ears. A drop of blood trickled from his nose. He wiped it away and said, "I won't release Moira whatever you say!"

"What the fuck!" Zach said and moved toward his brother. Ciaran knew Zach was using his sound wave to scan the room for the density of strange materials or sound sequences. Ciaran felt the air pressure around him increase and realized that Tadgh had dematerialized. In his dematerialized form, Tadgh could adjust himself to be at the same density level as the woman and would be able to see her.

"She didn't ask you to release Moira. She said Moira could help," Madeline said.

"You can hear her?" Ciaran asked.

"Yes. And it sounds like Zach and Tadgh are killing the woman. But I think she's a friend, Ciaran."

Ciaran looked into Madeline's eyes and could see the confidence and tenacity in them. "Let the woman go," he said.

Tadgh rematerialized. Zach still gazed at a corner of the room, but it appeared he had withdrawn his sound waves.

The corner screen switched on, and Jake, the current head of intelligence, came back on and said, "The astronomical paths are aligning, Ciaran. It's time to get ready."

"Would you be able to go straight to Tower One, Madeline?" Ciaran asked.

"What about our children?"

"You can't protect them even if you're going to the Daimon Gate. I'll send Tadgh and Jo."

"On it," Tadgh said.

"I'm ready, too," Jo seconded.

"Jo will be there if we need to handle anything technical. Tadgh will provide the muscle," Ciaran said.

"Thanks so much. Muscles are all I have?" Tadgh asked.

Ciaran glanced at Tadgh and continued, "Tadgh can also lead the gatekeepers and the guards of Daimon Gate. That will be more effective than any soldiers from the outside. I need you in Tower One, Madeline."

Madeline nodded. "Then I'll go." She logged off the screen.

"You can't send three Sciphils off during coronation."

Ciaran turned around to see Jake glaring at him from the screen. He met Ciaran's eyes without the slightest squirm.

"And you have justified reasons for that statement, Jake?" Ciaran asked.

"I looked up the power source in preparation for the energy connection and know you've sent Sciphil Eight away and set Tower Eight on automatic operation."

"You said towers can run on automatic for one unit. That will be enough for the coronation," Ciaran said.

"Yes, sir. But not three towers at once. The process requires energy exchanges between eight towers and the king tower. The maximum amount of energy that can be run on automatic is twenty-five percent. That's two towers, and even that is not ideal. But three towers off? It isn't going to work, sir."

Ciaran looked at his two experienced councillors, Pete and Janei. Pete raised his hands in the air and said, "I don't know—I've never been through a coronation before."

"The two coronations I've been to went smoothly," Janei said.

Ciaran looked at Jake. "So how do you know all this? I didn't see this information in any documentation."

"It's in an old manual of the central intelligence working procedures. I've been a deputy for this position for a long time. Sizx wasn't very open about information sources, so I had to learn it my way."

"Are you sure you can handle the process given you had to learn from manuals and have only been in the position for such a short time?"

"I am confident, sir. I have a photographic memory, and I can compute faster than the fastest machine in the station. I'm one hundred percent Eudaizian and not a lab project—like before."

"You're overstepping your bounds, Jake. It isn't your place to judge how Sizx was created," Janei scolded.

"He isn't judging anyone. Or any*thing* for that matter," Ciaran said, looking directly into Janei's eyes, causing her to look away. Then he continued, "Tadgh and Jo, would you please go to the Daimon Gate as planned?"

"Sure. But what about the twenty-five percent limit?" Tadgh asked.

"I'll reinstate Sciphil Eight," Ciaran said dryly and headed for the door.

"You just jailed the guy. Do you honestly think Aiden is going to crawl back and serve you with loyalty at this point?" Zach asked.

The corner of Ciaran's mouth quirked up in a faint smile. "Yes, I think he will."

Dan rushed over. "Ciaran, I need to speak to you." He lowered his voice. "In the last few days, I had a vision of a snake—a cobra to be precise."

Ciaran arched an eyebrow but continued to walk as he said, "I can set up a meeting with a shrink for you tomorrow."

"No, no. This isn't about me. It's about the coronation. I think the cobra has something to do with you."

"Look, Dan, I don't like snakes at all. But what we're dealing with right now is far more dangerous than a cobra. I understand the cobra has some mystical meanings. But unless you can give me more concrete information than what you saw in your dreams, I'll have to deal with it when I cross that bridge."

Dan shook his head.

"Very well then. Thanks for letting me know. Now get to Tower Five." Ciaran patted his shoulder and strode away.

CHAPTER 29

Gaia floated in a world of oblivion. It was dark but peaceful. But a corner of her mind wouldn't rest and wasn't susceptible to the drug-induced sleep she was in. She had things to do. She had a duty. She was on a mission. Then she heard her mother's voice calling her name from the darkness. Gentle but urging.

She opened her eyes and found the sheet tucked around her. She sensed her mother nearby. She sat up. The room was small, and the temperature was cool and pleasant. She tried to remember what had happened before. She recalled Ciaran taking her into the capsule and having a short conversation with her mother, but after that, the world became blurry.

"Gaia, we've got work to do. Are you a good girl?"

She turned in the direction of the voice. "Yes, Mother. I'm a good girl. What would you like me to do?"

***

Ciaran pulled out a chair and sat down opposite Aiden Felix, the detained Sciphil. It wasn't a cell but rather a small room where the lock code had been disabled so the system wouldn't recognize him.

"It'll be a long time before we can ever be friendly, Aiden."

"Does *never* qualify as a long time?" Aiden asked.

"I have a deal to make, and it doesn't involve friendship."

"Sounds promising."

Ciaran smiled. "After my coronation, I plan to split up your district and divide the citizens between the other territories. Based on my calculations, seven sub towers and a king tower make for the best composition of sustainable energy. Your district is the one I will let go."

"Don't you dare!" Aiden snarled and sprang out of his chair.

Ciaran remained still in his chair, staring hard, and the furious Sciphil stopped in his tracks. When Aiden again sat, Ciaran continued. "My offer to you is that I will leave District Eight intact as long as you are in power."

"What kind of deal is that? It's like raising the price of a product and then promoting a discount back down to normal price."

"When you get out of here, you can check the system. There has been a plan in place for some time. Perhaps you didn't notice because you were on your personal mission. But for now, if you take this deal, then you have to be in Tower Eight straight away and be cooperative throughout the coronation. If anything happens to me, there will be no Eudaiz and, therefore, no District Eight for you to govern."

Aiden grumbled some profanity.

Ciaran stood up. "I want to give you a chance. I want to see if you can truly be a good Sciphil before I decide to divide your district. Will you take this chance to prove yourself? Like it or not, in a unit or so, I will be king."

"I'll take the deal."

"Then you shall have it."

Ciaran nodded and left the room. Aiden trailed behind him.

***

Moira rushed through the dimensional gate to the basement underneath Sciphil Six residence. She had been hiding in iilos for such a long time and had traveled this route several times, but this time, it was different.

Excitement at the prospect of solving her five-hundred-year grievance tingled through her entire body. It was also a possibility to fulfill her promise to her husband. And the opportunity to see her daughter made her shiver. Five hundred years of living in despair. With every day that went by, her hope faded. She had no way to prove her fidelity to her late husband, but finding their daughter alive would give him a chance to rest in peace.

"Are you sure Gaia? Your mother knows about my daughter?"

"She said so. That's why she asked me to rescue you."

Moira grinned. "Then let's go."

Gaia shook her head. "No, we're not going to Xiilok."

"What do you mean? Your mother said she'll meet me there and tell me about my daughter."

"She told me to get you out of your dimension. But she will meet you at Tower Three, not in Xiilok."

"Tower Three? Where the coronation is going to be? Why would she want me to be there by myself? And without an army?"

Gaia grinned. "I *am* your army."

CHAPTER 30

This was the moment that would mark a significant change in his life—his coronation. Ciaran stepped out of the capsule and glanced up at his Tower Three, the king tower, savoring the last moment of being an ordinary man.

Jake had done a good job deploying the necessary forces to the right places. Ciaran smiled to himself and was glad he had trusted him. There were often moments in this universe when he doubted his ability to judge people's characters.

Eight thousand robotic soldiers surrounded the tower in the distance, and nearby, eight hundred man soldiers were lined up. The soldiers were solely for show, Ciaran thought. Once inside the tower, he would be alone and on his own, and he would have to manage this universe by himself. The lives of more than six hundred billion innocent civilians depended on a panel full of buttons and switches, and he was the only one who had full control over it.

He approached the tower and verified at the control panel. The nine gigantic walls slid into place to reveal the entrance. Ciaran walked in. The hallway widened for him.

Ciaran visited his key stone chamber first. Calling the room a chamber was an understatement. It was a gigantic dome, the key stone glass box soaring hundreds of feet above him. That box was where he would receive his eudqi—the multiversally powered life force of a king. It was the most precious gift Eudaiz had to offer him. His key stone glowed red, like the burning fires of heaven and hell combined.

On the wall was his king Sciphil sword, also shimmering in shades of crimson. His hand hovered over the blade, and the metal glowed in response. He touched the handle and staggered back as a jolt of energy surged through him. He had used this sword before—and had been stabbed by it before. He knew its power well and remembered how the metal felt when it pierced his skin. It had been Bran's sword when he used it. Now it was his, and it was taking his energy, combining with his eudqi, before it started giving.

Ciaran placed his hand on the handle again. It sucked a large amount of energy from him, sending him slumping to the floor. The sword vibrated and shot a beam, punching a large hole in the wall. "Idiot," Ciaran scolded himself aloud. He wasn't supposed to touch the sword before receiving the king eudqi. Today was a special day, and the energy worked differently. He stood up, adjusted up his clothes, and returned to the control chamber.

The lights and machines woke as he passed by. Ciaran verified, and rows and rows of monitors lit up. He stood at a half-moon-shaped console. In front of him were eighteen screens, eight of which showed individual Sciphil in their towers. An additional eight screens showed the central public square in each civilian district where billions of citizens gathered to celebrate the coronation. One screen was reserved as a direct communication channel with Jake at central intelligence, and the last one was the private master screen for the king tower.

The civilian screens showed massive crowds of citizens as they gathered in public squares with much anticipation. *They look happy,* he thought with a hint of anxiety as well as pride. He understood their emotion. They hadn't had a real connection with their king in the last thirty-three years. Any new leader would bring both new hope and a degree of anxiety. He could almost feel their anticipation seeping through the screens.

Soon he would connect the power to all stations. The correct alignment of the astrological elements would provide an incredible amount of energy. It would be a spectacular event.

"Central, are you ready?" he asked, looking at Jake's screen.

Jake's voice was full of confidence. "Yes, sir. All screens in all districts are engaged. You are on the direct communication channel to all citizens of Eudaiz. The public screens have been activated. You should be able to see and hear the citizen's reactions. Communication channels with all Sciphils at all six towers are connected. I'm testing the connections now. And we have two towers operating on automatic mode. Shall I perform the final communication check, sir?"

"Proceed," Ciaran said.

"Sciphil One, Madeline LeBlanc," Jake said.

"Hello," Madeline responded.

Ciaran smiled at Madeline, and she smiled back.

"Sciphil Two, Zach Flynn," Jake continued.

"Hello there," Zach responded.

"Sciphil Five, Dan Chandler."

"Yes, I'm ready."

"Sciphil Six, Janei Chatel."

"I'm ready," she said.

"Sciphil Eight, Aiden Felix."

A hesitation and then, "Of course I'm ready."

"Sciphil Nine, Pete Chandler."

"I can hear you loud and clear."

"Sciphil Seven, Tadgh LeBlanc, and Sciphil Four, Jo Cassidy, are absent. Their towers are in automatic operation mode, starting now," Jake said to Ciaran.

Ciaran nodded.

Then it seemed as it the air was vacuumed out of Eudaiz. For a moment, the silence was unbearable.

A chain of explosions came. They were so loud and powerful that the ground shook, the monitors bounced, and everyone and everything reeled from the effect. Regaining their footings, the citizens in the crowds looked around, confused.

Ciaran looked at the public screens and muttered, "So this is your game, Hoyt Flanagan. It isn't my children or my tower that you attack. You target my citizens. Bastard!"

In all districts, the civilians had started their celebratory ceremonies in front of the gigantic public screens. Eudaizians were everywhere. They were vulnerable.

The explosions had punched large holes in every district's protective walls. Through the holes, hundreds of Xiilok fighters stormed in. The streets filled with chaos and confusion, which quickly turned to fear as more and more fighters marched in.

Ordinary Eudaizian citizens had never seen a real war in their lives.

CHAPTER 31

Ciaran gazed at the public screen and knew innocent civilians were going to be slaughtered. He could see that even Janei, Pete, and Aiden—all experienced Sciphils—sweat in fear. They knew the implications.

"We have to rescue our citizens," Aiden said.

"But we have to stay in our towers during the coronation process," Pete objected.

"We can't just let them be killed," Janei said.

"The power for the coronation has been engaged, Ciaran. All towers have to be locked in now. What's your decision?" Jake asked.

"I can't send any Sciphils or guards out there. As soon as you leave your towers, you'll be attacked. If we lose a tower, we'll lose Eudaiz," Ciaran said.

"You're just worried about your coronation. I don't care what you say—I'm saving my citizens," Aiden said.

"Jake, lock all eight towers."

"Affirmative."

"Don't you dare! You can't lock us in!" Aiden punched the screen.

"I just did," Ciaran said with authority. "No one leaves their tower. We have to complete this coronation. If we get distracted, and the process fails, we'll lose Eudaiz."

"Civilians are dying, Ciaran. We swore to protect them," Pete said, wavering.

"We can only do that if we survive ourselves," Ciaran said and looked at Madeline. On the screen, she locked her gaze with his, giving him her complete support.

He turned to his public communication channel and activated it.

"My people, citizens of Eudaiz!" Ciaran's voice was broadcast loudly on the streets of Eudaiz, and his image appeared on all screens, both public and domestic.

Every civilian in Eudaiz stopped to listen to their king on the screen. Xiilok fighters on the street pushed and shoved, but the citizens resisted to hear what Ciaran had to say. In a panic, the fighters fired at the gigantic public screens, but the screens remained intact, made to be impervious to weapons.

Ciaran surveyed his people from the screens. He gazed at the hundreds of faces of Eudaizian citizens on the screens. "Today, I'm supposed to swear to protect Eudaizians as your king, but I'm afraid I may not be able to do so."

People were confused. They looked around in disbelief.

Ciaran continued, "I cannot protect you if you are not willing to protect yourselves. We created the technology to protect you hundreds of years ago, but the devil has now broken through your protective shields. The devil is now standing right next to you in your own districts. I and the eight Sciphils are very far away. We will get to you, but I'm afraid we will be too late."

The crowds rumbled, and people became more puzzled. Some started to shove the fighters in anger. The fighters fired at the screens once more, but their weapons still caused no damage. A small group of fighters shot into the air as a warning and then into a group of the Eudaizians who pushed back at them. The citizens toppled like trees. Civilians screamed and pushed. Some tried to run away, and the fighters mowed them down with their weapons. The chaos intensified.

Ciaran shouted out from the screen. "Do not run!"

But people ran. And the fighters fired.

Ciaran yelled. "Stop!"

One group of citizens in one of the districts listened to Ciaran's instructions and stopped. Others did the same.

"If you run, they'll shoot you from behind. Turn around and face them."

Some of the people turned around.

"Turn around!" Ciaran commanded.

They obeyed.

The fighters were stunned by the combined force of the people. They withdrew slightly.

"You were told to be good citizens. Never harm others, never profit from others. But up to this point, you have not faced evil. Right now, directly in front of you—this is evil."

The fighters opened fire on the people standing in the front, and the crowds started to retreat.

Ciaran continued. "They have weapons, but there are only a few hundred of them. We have more than *six hundred billion* Eudaizians. How can you let a few fighters intimidate you?"

The fighters fired again. Some people in the crowds cried out.

"Don't just stand there! Advance! If you advance, they will have no choice but to retreat."

The fighters fired their weapons again, but neither civilians nor fighters were advanced.

"If you do nothing, they will kill you. Think about those you love. Your husband. Your wife. Your children. They will destroy and enslave generations of you and your family. They *will* kill you. Are you going to let that happen?"

No response. The fighters stopped, anticipating the outcome of Ciaran's words.

"Will you allow them to destroy Eudaiz?" Ciaran asked.

Someone said, "No." Another voice echoed the response.

"Say *no* for me. All of you. Say *no*!" Ciaran's voice blasted from the speakers on the screen.

A thunderous *no* split the air and shook the universe.

"Look at them! Look at the devil and say *kill*!" Ciaran shouted.

"Kill!" They could feel the ground shake. The civilians repeated it. *"Kill! Kill! Kill!"*

"Advance. Crush them!" Ciaran commanded.

The crowds charged the fighters. On the screens, Ciaran could see the fear in the fighters' eyes. They couldn't shoot, couldn't run. Obviously, they couldn't pray because there was no God in Eudaiz. There was nothing in any universe that could save them at that moment.

Oceans of people in every district marched right over the fighters. When the waves of civilians had passed, there was nothing left but black puddles on the ground. Some evaporated into thin air, and some filled with swimming worms.

The people then turned back to the screens—looked at him, their king—and cheered. Ciaran smiled at his people and could swear he felt the ground shaking and the air vibrating from the force of their will.

Then the smiles faded from the faces of the Eudaizians on the screen. As they turned around, Ciaran could see more soldiers marching in via the holes to replace the ones trampled by the crowds. These looked more vicious, more intelligent, and much more dangerous.

Ciaran knew he couldn't issue his citizens into another bloodbath. He could pull off that stunt once, but not twice. They needed more than just moral support. He had to take action himself. If the Xiilok soldiers forced their way all the way to the back of the line, women and children would die, but not before they'd been forced to bathe in the blood of their men at the front.

He looked at Madeline, whose tears were streaming down her face. His wife knew him. She knew his intentions. She wouldn't tell him no because it would be morally wrong. But she was hurt.

"I'm sorry, Madeline," he said and turned toward the public screens.

"What are you doing? What the fuck do you think you're doing?" Zach asked.

"I know what you're capable of, but that's foolish, Ciaran," Pete said.

"Insane," Janei agreed.

"If you do it, you will have my loyalty for the rest of my life," Aiden said.

Ciaran nodded at his Sciphils, stopped to look at Madeline a moment longer, and then turned around and entered his glass chamber.

CHAPTER 32

Inside the glass chamber, the control panel was different. The key stone above him was glowing red as if ready for the coronation. On a corner monitor, an interactive map was showing the process of the astronomical movements of the cosmic energy as it lined up for the coronation. It looked like a mystical galaxy, blanketed in a dust storm of particles and electric currents. The moment of the coronation was approaching. He had to take action before it happened.

"Jake, engage the power of all district protective shields into the source of Tower Three's weapon."

Jake stared at the screen. Inside the glass chamber, Ciaran didn't have a connection with other Sciphils' screens, but he could see the main screen through the glass of the chamber. There seemed to be a discussion going on between the active Sciphils, but he couldn't hear what they were saying.

"Sir, you want me to connect you to the weaponry system?"

"Yes."

"Can we do this after the coronation?" Jake asked.

Ciaran glanced at the public screens outside and saw that the Xiilok and Black Rock soldiers had started their slaughter. He looked at the interactive map of the movements in the cosmos and could tell the coronation wasn't ready. He glanced at the public screens again and could see more and more people falling on the streets as every second passed.

"We have to do it now, Jake. That's an order."

"Affirmative." Jake looked down to his panel and executed a command.

***

From Tower One, Madeline asked, "Jake, what does Ciaran want?" She could see Jake switching from one communication channel to another. The other Sciphils could hear and respond to the conversation between Madeline and Jake because they were on the same Sciphil channel.

"Ciaran will use the weaponry system in the protective shields of all districts to shoot at the intruders," Jake responded.

"That's what the weapon is for, isn't it?" Madeline asked.

"Except that it doesn't have its own ammunition. Eudaiz is a peaceful universe," said Janei.

"So how will Ciaran use it?" Zach asked.

"It shoots the energy from the king tower."

"And that will be strong enough to kill all these creatures at once?" Dan asked.

"Yes, but the king tower's energy connects directly with the king's energy," Pete said.

"Ciaran could blast his mind blade. It can kill a few hundred in a district," Madeline said the paused. "But not all eight districts at once."

"Plus, he's only a man. He doesn't have any king power yet," Aiden said. When Madeline glared at him, he shrugged. "That's why I said he'll have my lifelong loyalty if he does this. He knew the risks when he made this decision."

"Can I talk to Ciaran, Jake?" Madeline asked.

"I'm sorry, but there's no direct connection to the glass chamber from outside," Jake responded.

"Are you saying he might die doing this?" Madeline asked.

"The possibility is stronger than *might*," Aiden said.

"We can help," Pete said quietly.

"I am on it, Sciphil Nine. Please give instructions," Jake said, his eyes sparking with anticipation.

***

Inside the glass chamber, Ciaran could see that the connection with the district weaponry system had been engaged. A flashing red palm sign glowed, demanding his print for activation.

He turned to look at Madeline's screen. She was busy and appeared to be in a heated debate with the other Sciphils, but he couldn't hear her. He turned to his panel and hovered his palm over it.

"Jake, can you connect me to the public channel so I can give the Eudaizians instructions?"

Silence.

Ciaran looked at Jake's screen. He looked as if he was entering a command, but there was no sound coming from his screen.

"Jake!"

Jake looked up and flicked on the sound.

"Yes, Ciaran."

"Did you just switch channels?"

"No, Ciaran. I was checking the connections."

"Can you connect me to the public screens so I can give instructions to the civilians before I blast the weapon?"

"Sorry, Ciaran. That can't be done from inside the glass chamber."

"All right. Can you pass my instructions on to them? Tell the women and children to retreat from the front line, and ask the men to stay. Those who stay need to know they may die—the blasts can't discriminate between Eudaizians and creatures. If they stay, they must know that they can't turn and run. If they do, the creatures will give chase, and the blasts will kill them all. Am I understood?"

"Yes, I'll do that right now."

Jake switched to another channel, and Ciaran could no longer hear him. He looked through the glass wall and could see the civilians on the screen reacting to his instructions. They formed lines and withdrew in an orderly fashion given the chaos of the situation.

In a short moment, Jake switched back. Ciaran nodded. He fixed his stance and placed his palm on the flashing panel.

The suction when he did so was immediate and mind-blowing. His left hand became glued to the panel as his life force was sucked out of his body. He braced his other hand on the console to remain upright and alert and focused. He wielded his mind blades and channeled them into the weaponry system.

He knew the risks, but he thought he could leverage the power of his mind blades to make up for the lack of king power. He peered out to the public screen and saw the first blast come from the protective shield of District Five. He couldn't control the order of the blasts nor how much force went into each.

Half of the fighters were blown into pieces. He could see he needed another blast there, so he wielded his blade again. It came. It shook the district, graded the ground, and blew up the rest of the creatures in District Five—and half of the front-line civilians.

He needed to move to the next district. Ciaran realized he couldn't move. Blood trickled from his nose, and his head felt like it weighed more than a mountain. He had known this process would drain him of all his life force, but he didn't think he would go so quickly.

He had to save more than one district.

He tried again. It didn't work. Nothing happened.

He realized how ordinary the energy of a human was, regardless how talented and resourceful the person. Even a child conceived in the Red Stage of the Daimon Gate—one of the best beings in the cosmos—was still a human.

His knees buckled. He grabbed the console to regain his balance. He looked outside again, but his vision was too blurry to see anything.

***

From outside Tower Three, Moira pulled Gaia back by the hand. They stood behind the line of soldiers surrounding the tower. More than anyone, Moira knew the soldiers were just for show. They couldn't help with what was happening inside, and they couldn't assist in the coronation.

"Gaia, you said your mother would be here. Where is she?"

Gaia tilted her head and appeared to be listening, then she said, "Mother said if you can take me inside Tower Three, I can help Ciaran."

"I know you're a conduit and can help draw energy. I don't know much about Ciaran, but I'm sure he won't use a child in battle. But more importantly, I don't have a permit to get inside Tower Three."

Gaia looked up at Moira. "Mother says you can get in if you want to."

"Your mother has to give me a very good reason to do that, Gaia."

Gaia waited. She glanced around. Then she looked up at Moira. "Mother has left us."

CHAPTER 33

The control panel in front of him became blurrier by the second. Then a glowing green panel with a flashing palm sign appeared. He might have been imagining it, but he thought the text below it said, "Connect to the power of eight towers."

Without hesitation, he hit it with his right palm.

An ocean of energy flew into him from behind his head. His vision cleared up. In the reflection on the glass wall, he could see his key stone spinning and a glowing funnel of energy pouring down on him. He glanced at the Sciphils screens outside and saw all of them standing in front of their control panels.

The ground shook. The district screens showed a chain of blasts from every protective shield. Creature's bodies were blown into pieces.

For a long moment, Eudaiz was lost in a haze of confusion and chaos.

Then the dust settled. The sound quieted. People stood up and started taking inventory. The bodies and body parts of creatures were everywhere. Fallen Eudaizian men were among them.

The creatures' bodies evaporated, and the bodies of the Eudaizians glowed brightly and then vanished. It was their tradition—their essences would be absorbed into objects that their loved ones knew well.

On the screens, Eudaiz had returned to its peaceful quietness.

"We won," Ciaran said with relief.

He pushed open the door of the glass chamber and collapsed onto the floor before pulling himself to his feet and walking to the control panel. He spoke into the communicator that went out to the public screens. "My proud citizens of Eudaiz, we are victorious. Congratulations!"

And then there was another loud explosion on the public screens, but this time, it was the vocal explosion of joy, excitement, and pride.

Ciaran turned toward his councillors and found them smiling at him—even Aiden.

"Thank you. I couldn't have done it without your help," Ciaran said.

"Well, you trusted us enough to hook up with the energy we gave. So that's an improvement." Janei smiled.

"We're proper Sciphils. You are not yet king. If you hadn't been brave enough to start it, I wouldn't have given you my support," Aiden said.

"It was Pete's idea," Madeline said.

"Thanks again," Ciaran said.

"Do you have enough left in your tank to finish the coronation? It will be a hell of a process," Zach asked.

"There's only one way to find out." Ciaran smiled and glanced at the interactive map. The critical time was approaching. "We're almost there," he said and noticed Dan's scowl. He recalled Dan's mention of a vision he had of a cobra. By the looks of it, he must have had another one.

Then Ciaran turned toward Madeline and saw that the smile had faded from her face. He turned to Dan to ask a question but couldn't because the Sciphil screens flickered and blinked off one by one. Madeline had left her control panel before her screen went blank. He turned toward Jake's screen and found him hitting buttons wildly and frantically working on commands to correct the disconnection. Before Ciaran could ask a question, Jake's screen went black.

The air in the control chamber grew colder. An eerie, chilling breeze brushed behind him, and at the same time, Ciaran heard a chuckle.

He knew that chuckle.

Ciaran turned around. "Hoyt Flanagan," he said with a forced smile. "So this is your end game. A one-on-one with me."

"You're spent. It won't be much of a fight. But I'll enjoy the victory regardless. Didn't expect this, did you?"

"No, indeed, I did not. You got me on this move," Ciaran said.

"I certainly did, and I'll soon be rewarded. Your throne. Your life. Your wife... I can taste it."

A loud bang came from the security mechanism of the of the gates, and the tower rumbled. The noise echoed through the grand hall. The nine gigantic gates started spinning. Hoyt had triggered them so that no one could get in or out unless Ciaran took them through.

Ciaran shook his head. "You made me use up my energy. You cut off my communication channels. And now you're attempting to isolate me from outside help. Do you fear me that much?"

"Five hundred years of failure has taught me to be cautious. What does a kid like you know?"

"I know for a fact that nothing in this multiverse would make me stoop that low. Not even the kingship."

Hoyt laughed. "I wouldn't do all of this just for the kingship. I've traveled the cosmos. I've been to heaven and hell. Where have you been? What do you know, Ciaran? But you're right. Nothing would make a person stoop so low. But thanks to the LeBlancs, I am no longer a person, no longer human. For me, anything and everything is worth ending the LeBlancs right here and now." He moved closer to Ciaran and repeated, "Everything will be worth it. And I will enjoy every nanosecond that you are in pain."

"Why not simply put a bullet in my head and take the throne. Wouldn't that be easier?"

Hoyt laughed. "First of all, there are no bullets in Eudaiz. You really must let go of such earthly expressions, Ciaran. Secondly, a man has his pride. Killing you quickly would be too easy. I haven't had a chance for a one-on-one with you and will enjoy beating you up."

"In that form?" Ciaran looked Hoyt up and down. "How could you get any satisfaction out of this, even if you win?"

"As I said, my satisfaction will come from your pain. So endure it." He charged at Ciaran.

CHAPTER 34

England 1605

Hoyt sauntered into the mouth of the cave in the woods after a day on horseback from Mortlake. Not that he couldn't afford a carriage. He enjoyed riding. It kept him fit and agile. Plus, it was the only outdoor activity he'd had lately with his busy schedule.

The weather wasn't perfect, but he couldn't complain. His horse, however, did. If his horse knew a fraction of what the weather was like in the Irish Highland where he had trained winter after winter, it wouldn't moan.

But although the weather didn't bother him, Hoyt disliked the location. Something about the cave and the timing of the gathering bothered him.

He was a trained sorcerer. He knew he was young and had a lifetime in front of him to practice his craft. He was talented and qualified enough to leave his clan and build his own branch of sorcery. But sorcery wasn't enough for him, and Ireland was too small to contain his ambition.

He traveled to London and applied to be an alchemy apprentice for John Dee, a famous astrologer, alchemist, and an adviser to the Queen. He wanted a taste of science and of what alchemy could offer him. He didn't care about making precious metal. He was more intrigued by the science behind the spiritual matter. It was an oxymoron to many, but an amazing possibility to him.

At the alchemic laboratory, he met Moira. She was an acquaintance of John Dee and had a strong interest in alchemy. Her beauty captured his attention the very first moment they met, and her intelligence put him—a cocky young Irish sorcerer—in his place.

Well, perhaps not so cocky after all when he discovered that Moira was Pierre LeBlanc's wife. The LeBlancs were one of the richest families in France. When his feelings for Moira grew from a crush to an obsession, he decided to leave.

Then he got an invitation from John Dee for a gathering there. He only accepted because he knew Moira would be there. He had eyes and ears on her everywhere she went. His obsession was overwhelming and all-encompassing.

What he didn't expect was the sight of Moira walking in with her husband. His intelligence had informed him that Pierre was on a business trip in Spain. *Damn!* he cursed to himself, giving the expected cursory nod toward the couple.

A servant delivered a message saying John Dee was late and would arrive shortly. In the meantime, food and wine were served.

More people arrived, and Hoyt grew increasingly uncomfortable with the whole event. He saw John Dee's relatives and acquaintances and their servants. But his patience hit the limit when Edward Kelley's family arrived. Edward and John had been in a lifetime dispute over the gold-making business. Hoyt wasn't sure if they had even made any gold. But the rivalry between the two families was deep.

When Hoyt assembled the relevant facts together, everyone in the cave knew an aspect of John Dee's life, one he didn't care for. For Hoyt, he walked into John's lab and saw him cursing a failed experiment he needed to present the Queen. Hoyt knew he had done that presentation. Which meant he cheated the Queen in his presentation.

He didn't know about which of secrets others had held against John Dee, but the gathering was not coincidental.

But it was too late.

Lightning struck at the entrance of the cave and caused stones to collapse, blocking their way out. Only John Dee would be able to calculate the odds and predict such a natural disaster.

Then the storm came. It was vicious. But the natural disaster wasn't the killer—the dimensional hole opening right beneath their feet that flung them into the emptiness was.

They floated in the oblivion for a long time before they landed at the Daimon Gate. They went through all the challenges together to get to Eudaiz. Only the best ten of them survived—the first nine Sciphils of Eudaiz and Moira.

Hoyt enjoyed it the most because he was now legitimately working side by side with Moira's husband. He was her equal, and he got to see her every day on council business.

But one day, he decided that standing on the sidelines wasn't enough. She rejected him multiple times, and he made winning her his life's mission—one he had never been able to accomplish.

Over time, his mission had changed from getting Moira to taking power away from the LeBlancs. He had tried and failed many times on both missions.

Until now.

He was so close he could smell the success.

CHAPTER 35

Ciaran braced his hands on the console for balance and calculated how long he would last in a hand-to-hand fight with Hoyt. Not long at all, he thought. He had to weaken Hoyt somehow. He made a move as if he was charging toward the king Sciphil sword on the wall. As he predicted, Hoyt gave him a hard kick and beat him to the sword.

Hoyt grabbed the sword. As it had done to Ciaran before, the sword drew a large amount of energy from Hoyt and sent him staggering to the floor. Ciaran grabbed his daggers from the console, flew toward Hoyt, and stabbed forward.

Hoyt howled in pain and kicked Ciaran away. Ciaran knew too well that he couldn't kill Hoyt with mere daggers. He was beyond the realm of a human being. A physical weapon wouldn't do much damage at all, but he wanted to weaken him.

And he did.

"Daggers?" Hoyt said in disdain.

Ciaran shrugged. "Whatever works."

Hoyt charged at Ciaran bare-handed. Ciaran dropped the daggers to the floor and met Hoyt in the middle of the grand hall. They matched each other blow for blow, kick for kick.

The exchange sapped the energy from them both. They dropped to the floor, drawing in heavy breaths. Ciaran glanced at the interactive map and could see the astrological elements had moved even closer. Hoyt saw it, too, and he knew what it meant.

Ciaran stood up. "If you want the throne, then fight like a king."

They flew at each other again.

***

Moira was getting more agitated by the second. "If your mother isn't back soon, I'm taking you to my residence. Can you see the sparks at the top of the tower? There's a fight going on inside. The protective shields are spinning. If you try to walk through those walls, they will grind you into dust."

"But Mother said you can take me inside to help Ciaran. She said you know the way."

"*That* is the way. If we walk in, the walls will grind us into nothing more than black pepper."

Gaia pouted, and tears gleamed in her eyes.

Moira crouched down. "Look, Gaia, I know you want to please your mother. But I'm sure she wouldn't want you to die doing whatever it is she wants. Ciaran can handle himself. He always has."

"No, he can't this time. He needs help. That's what Mother said." Her tears started again. "I can't disappoint her. She'll leave me forever."

Moira pulled Gaia into her arms. "I heard about your father. You poor child. I'll take care of you."

A capsule flew over, hovered, and landed. Madeline darted out. Robert climbed clumsily over the steps after locking the capsule.

"I have to get inside. Ciaran needs me," Madeline said.

"How do you know?"

"He's my husband. Of course I know."

Madeline could see the pain in Moira's eyes, but she wasn't sorry for having said so. It was the truth, and she needed to push hard to get Moira to help her to get inside the tower.

"Hoyt is inside. Ciaran has used up all of his energy saving the citizens in the districts. He's no match for Hoyt now," Madeline said.

"He killed my father. Take me in. Take me in." Gaia started to cry again.

The commander of the soldiers outside the tower approached. "Is there anything I can do to help, Sciphil One?" he asked.

"I needed to get inside."

He shook his head. "You know we can't. Even when the walls aren't spinning, we have no access."

Madeline heard the voice of Gaia's mother in her head again. She turned toward Moira. "Gaia's mother told me she'll fight Hoyt to the death inside the tower. She said I can help her, but only if you stop the walls and let me in."

"I don't know how!" Moira exclaimed.

"She said if you want to see her one last time before she dies, before you lose her once again, then you have to stop the walls."

"Why would I want to see—" Moira's voice trailed off. "Lose her once again?"

"That's what she said."

Moira looked at the tower. "No, I won't lose her again," she said and strode toward the tower. Madeline asked the commander to take care of Gaia and followed her.

"Madeline, I want to go in with you!" Gaia shouted.

"Let me see first how we get in. Then I promise I'll come back and take you in. Please be good and stay here, Gaia."

Gaia nodded, wiped her tears, and stayed where she was.

Running right behind Moira, Madeline looked at the nine gigantic slabs of concrete as they spun in circles. "Do you have a plan?"

"No. But I know the pattern and what it takes to get through the gate."

"How?"

"Because I helped design it. You stay on my left and one step behind me. Always. Got that?"

"Yes."

Moira concentrated on the spinning walls. While Madeline saw nothing different, Moira pulled back slightly and then charged straight into the concrete. A slight gap opened very quickly, and she sneaked into the first layer. The first piece of concrete hit her and stopped for a fraction of a second. Madeline jumped to Moira's left.

Moira fell but jumped up instantly, charging into the second layer. It hit her and stopped. Madeline jumped to Moira's left. The layer behind Madeline started spinning again.

Now Madeline realized Moira's plan. She would be a human shield for Madeline through the nine layers. It was too late to turn back.

CHAPTER 36

Madeline jumped out from the last layer of steel doors, and Moira slumped to the floor. She was no more than a pile of bloody clothes. Madeline knew there couldn't be a bone in Moira's body that wasn't broken. She helped Moira up so they could head toward the main chamber, and they heard the faint sounds of a scuffle.

Madeline and Moira arrived at the main chamber to find two identical versions of Ciaran fighting.

Now everything made perfect sense to Madeline—the planting of Sizx into their journey, the red herrings, the plotted attacks, and the sorcery tricks to pull information from Ciaran's mind. All of it was to get as much information about Ciaran as possible so that Hoyt could slide into his skin and become the king. He would deal with the aftermath later. What a perfect plan.

She had no way to tell them apart. She bet if she tested their DNA, it would be identical, too.

Madeline set Moira down, leaning her against a wall.

The two versions of Ciaran were so identical physically and psychologically that they matched each other blow for blow in the fight and had beaten each other bloody. Both of them could barely move, and neither would give up. They were going to beat each other to death.

Madeline pulled out her Sciphil sword. "All right, both of you, put your weapons down! In your current condition, one swing of this sword, and both of your heads will be on the floor." Both men put their daggers down.

"Stand far apart, please. I know that one of you is Hoyt Flanagan." Madeline stuck her sword out and cut the Ciaran on her right on the arm.

"Sorry if it's you, Ciaran, but I have to be able to tell."

The two men chuckled nervously.

"What was the dessert we had on our first dinner date?" Madeline asked.

"Cheesecake," they chorused.

"What animal do you fear most?"

"Worms," they said simultaneously.

"What color is the stone of the wedding ring you gave me in the Daimon Gate?"

"I didn't give you a ring," both of the men said.

"Stop talking!" Madeline snarled. She looked at Moira. "Hoyt knows everything about Ciaran. Ciaran knows nothing about Hoyt, but you know him. Can you ask them some questions?"

Moira nodded. "In the cave outside Mortlake, you protected me from a falling rock, and I thought you were a gentleman."

The men's faces were icy.

Moira continued. "When you asked me to leave my husband and go with you to Black Rock, I thought you were crazy. But I did move based on that brave attempt."

There was no reaction.

"I considered your proposal, and that very thought contaminated our consummation in the Daimon Gate." Tears rolled down Moira's face. Moira had told her that story. But for her to talk about it as if her infidelity was fact was unacceptable.

The men still gave no reaction.

"It's not worth it, Moira. Please stop talking. You were faithful to your husband, and there's no way I would let you sound like a traitor to lure Hoyt out. He's a coward. He won't do it."

Then she heard Gaia's mother's voice, "Hoyt, you're a coward. You think you killed me? You didn't. You destroyed my physical presence, but you didn't destroy my mind. The mind lives forever. You won't have a mind after this. I will kill it."

The men in front of her slumped to the ground, covering their ears while blood flowed from their noses.

"Please don't. Whoever you are, don't speak to them. Their make is identical. You'll kill them both," Madeline said.

"Can she hear me, Madeline?" Moira asked.

"I think so."

"Iilos, is that you? You are my Iilos, aren't you?"

The woman's voice intensified with every word. "I followed you all over the cosmos, Hoyt. I never had a chance to kill you. Now you've taken Ciaran's form. Stay there and die. Now you know what it's like to have your body taken from you."

"No, no, Iilos, don't do this. You'll kill Ciaran as well," Madeline said.

Blood leaked from both men's ears as they rolled in agony on the floor.

"Come out and leave, Hoyt. I promise I won't kill you," Madeline continued. "Your parents helped build Eudaiz, Iilos. Whatever the problem you had with them, you're killing the king-to-be of Eudaiz."

"She left me. My mother left me with him," Iilos wailed.

"No, she never left you. Hoyt used magic on your parents and took you from them," Madeline said.

"Iilos, how could you think I left you?" Moira cried out. "I stayed here all these years hoping that one day I would find you and bring you back. I promised your father."

"Hoyt told me you left me. He said you didn't love me. He said I was his daughter with you!" Iilos shouted.

The two men on the floor writhed and blood trickled from their mouths now.

Madeline repeated what Iilos had just said to Moira. "Moira, don't let her do this."

"I can't hear you, Iilos. I want to hear you myself. I want to see you," Moira begged.

Moira pulled her sleeve up, revealing something that looked like a small bracelet.

"Mother, don't do this," Iilos said.

"She told you to stop doing what you're doing," Madeline translated, but Moira had already peeled off the bracelet.

As soon as the bracelet left her arm, five hundred years of time caught up with her. Moira said, "This is the dimensional resistance. It kept me alive all these years, but it stopped me from seeing dematerialized creatures. When I found that elusive dimension and named it after you, Iilos, I hid there and waited. I looked everywhere for you. I didn't know he had destroyed your form, and you couldn't cross to my dimension."

Madeline could tell that Iilos had switched the speech frequency because the men had stopped bleeding and were regaining some movement. She held up her sword, pointing it at them.

"Please let me hear you, my daughter," Moira cried. Moira looked about a hundred and fifty years old now and was fading quickly.

"He burned my body, Mother. He locked me up. When I was eighteen, I could detach my mind from my body. I wandered around looking for you. He found out, and he burned my body so I couldn't get back. Mother, please don't die!" Iilos cried.

"Don't cry my darling." She held out the bracelet. "I want to see you, Iilos. It will give you back your form."

"I've been like this for a long time. I don't need a form. Please put it back. I don't want you to die, Mother."

"The only reason I have lived this long is to find you. Now I have. I want to be with your father. I know you want to kill Hoyt, but this isn't the right way. You can't kill Ciaran and destroy Eudaiz because it's your father's legacy. Let me see you before I go."

One of the Ciarans sat up, and Madeline kicked him back to the ground. She tried not to think about which one she may have assaulted.

Moira held out the bracelet. "It was an experiment when your father made it. He was a genius. I changed some elements so that it alters your material mass and adapts your body accordingly to the changes of time, space, and dimension. You will never die or grow old naturally."

There was the sound of the bracelet snapping onto something. The image of a young woman gradually appeared. She had stunning, long red hair, milky skin, striking blue eyes, and the face of an angel—she was a younger image of Moira.

"You are beautiful, Iilos," Moira whispered. There wasn't much of her left. "Do you know what your name means?"

Iilos gathered Moira into her arms. "It's the Greek word for sunflower."

"That's right..." Moira smiled and faded away another hundred years. Then her body glowed and disintegrated into nothingness.

At the other end of the room, the two men had stood up, and Madeline was swinging the sword back and forth between them. The men were weak. She could cut them both down, but she couldn't take the chance of knocking out the real Ciaran. It wasn't for sentimental reasons. She'd knocked him out cold previously when the situation required. But now, she needed to let him complete the coronation.

The two versions of Ciaran locked their eyes on each other.

In the corner of the room, a screen flashed and came alive.

CHAPTER 37

The men engaged in their fight again and moved toward the glass chamber. Madeline looked at the interactive map. She didn't need to read the technical information to know that the elements for the moment of coronation were quickly clicking into place. She knew that if either one of the two versions of Ciaran got into the glass chamber, the system would verify him because their profiles were identical.

"Don't move any closer. Don't make me swing my sword!" Madeline darted in front of the glass chamber to prevent either of the men from entering.

From the screen at the corner of the room, Jo's voice came out. "Ciaran, are you there? Sorry, I can't get the visual working—"

"I'm here," both men said.

"Hmm, there's an echo from your end. But as long as you can hear me, it'll do," Jo said.

Madeline chuckled. *Very smart Ciaran*, she thought. He'd sent Jo and Tadgh on different missions as opposed to the Daimon Gate. It would help her tell the two versions of Ciaran in front of her apart. Whatever it was that Ciaran had sent Jo and Tadgh to do, it would hurt Hoyt. Badly.

She studied the men's expressions. One wrong flicker across either of their faces, and she would cut that person's head off.

Jo continued, "We swung by the Daimon Gate. It's all good there. Your children are coming out early, and your parents know it. Tadgh instructed the palace guards to protect the host residence. Security is tight. I don't think an army of any kind could get through. They also alerted the nine thousand gatekeepers. So the short version is that your children are safe."

Madeline narrowed her eyes as both men showed signs of relief in identical ways. *Damn!*

Jo proceeded with her report. "Then we went to Xiilok and Black Rock. Your experimental compass worked while all other navigational technology failed. And you nailed it, Ciaran. You correctly marked Hoyt's military bases on the compass. The technology was amazing. Hoyt must have been very busy in the last hundred years or more. The majority of the soldiers at the bases were deployed elsewhere when we arrived. So we blew up all the bases and destroyed the technology and the remaining housekeeping creatures."

Madeline focused hard on the men's faces. The real Ciaran would smile at this success, and Hoyt would likely cry. Hoyt now had no body and no home. His lifetime's work had just been burned to ashes.

In front of her, both men smiled and said, "Well done, Jo and Tadgh."

"Goddamnit, you're a coward, Hoyt!" Madeline exclaimed.

"Hoyt? What are you talking about?" Jo asked.

Then Tadgh's voice, "Madeline, why is Hoyt inside Tower Three? And why are you there? The system requires six Sciphils in their towers during the coronation process."

"That's why you and Jo need to get back to your towers as soon as possible."

They heard Tadgh cursing, and then the screen was turned off. As soon as that happened, the two Ciaran clones engaged in fighting again.

"Stop! Stop fighting, you two!" Madeline yelled at them. "Stand apart. The children are safe. And that means Ciaran will have an heir. So I can afford to cut both your heads off right now!"

Both men chuckled.

Damn it! Admittedly, she was just bluffing— and she hadn't done very well.

"There is one person who can tell them apart." It was Iilos, who had been solemnly absorbing the pain of losing her mother. She approached and looked at both men. She looked into Madeline's eyes and said, "It's Lyla."

CHAPTER 38

Iilos raised her hand and said something in a strange language that sounded something like singing. On the floor, the image of a thirteen-year-old girl appeared. She wore a white dress and glowed like an angel. She curtsied at Iilos and spoke with a French accent, "Teacher, I'm glad to be able to see you in person. Thank you for summoning me. I have been waiting for this moment for a long time."

Madeline kept one eye focused on both men, looking for even a single hair out of place.

Iilos said, "Lyla is a soul trader. Her natural life on Earth was meant to be cut short by illness, but I took her in as my student and trained her. With the right magic, incorporating the right elements, she would be able to trade a part of her soul to save a life. If she chooses the right partner, her trade will ensure that a part of her soul lives forever, and that she can make a difference in the world that has denied her of a longer natural life."

Lyla turned toward the two men. "Ciaran," she said.

"Yes," the men chorused and then glared at each other.

Iilos continued calmly, "Ciaran sealed a deal when he said the spell. A part of Lyla's soul is connected to Ciaran's soul. Each individual has a soul that can't be replicated in any form. So if the two of you say the spell right now, Lyla can tell which one of you is her partner."

Madeline interrupted, "No, no, Iilos. Hoyt tried to pry the spell out of Ciaran's mind twice. Ciaran had given it up in Xiilok. Hoyt knew the spell. If they say the same spell, can Lyla really tell? Are you sure?"

Iilos frowned. "I'm sure."

"Have you tried this before?" Madeline asked.

"No."

"Then you're not sure."

"Do you have a different idea, Madeline?"

Madeline shifted her stance, still holding tight to her sword. "What if...I kill them both? Then Lyla can save the real Ciaran, right? The one and only Ciaran with the correct soul. Is that how you said it works?"

Iilos was reluctant. Both men turned and looked at Madeline. "That's a wicked idea, Madeline. I like it," they said.

"Stop talking, or I'll kill you for real," she snarled and swung the sword. Then Madeline looked at Iilos, and she could tell Iilos wasn't sure at all about either of the solutions.

"Lyla, if they both say the spell, will you be able to tell them apart?" Iilos asked.

"I believe so. Because the spell from the real Ciaran will be spoken from his soul. That will not be fake."

Iilos raised an eyebrow at Madeline, waiting. Madeline swung her sword, pointing from one man to the other. "Okay, say it."

Both men staggered back to avoid the razor sharp tip of the sword.

Madeline swung her sword again. "Say it, or I cut both your heads off."

The men closed their eyes and murmured something. Immediately, a shriek from hell echoed throughout the room, and a cold breeze rushed in.

The man on the right grabbed his neck as if strangled. He gasped for air, trying to break free. He struggled, he shuddered, and then he turned into the ancient form of Hoyt Flanagan. His face cracked, his eyes bled, his body expanded. He grew bigger and bigger. He roared and swatted at invisible creatures swooping around them.

"You liar!" Hoyt roared.

Ciaran stood, looking at the dying Hoyt in front of him. "Five hundred years of failure should have taught you better, Hoyt. You should understand that a LeBlanc will never give up. When you rip a spell out of my mind, you should remember I'm one of the stubborn LeBlancs that have defeated you many times. You asked for a soul-trading spell. I'll give it to you. But Lyla isn't your soul-trading partner. It's Death."

"You made a deal with Death! You'll pay!" Hoyt screamed.

"No, I didn't make that deal. You just did."

Hoyt grew and grew. His girth blew out waves of black dust that swirled around the room like a small tornado.

"You're wrong Ciaran. What I don't have, nobody can. That's the trait of the Flanagans."

Hoyt's body exploded into thousands of particles. It swirled in the air and, in lightning speed, formed into a gigantic cobra. The snake hovered in the air and flew at Ciaran, who had no weapon in hand.

Madeline swung her sword, cutting the snake in half in its flying path, but it was too fast. The head of the snake still darted toward Ciaran.

He staggered back and ducked aside, but it was too late. The gigantic venomous fangs stabbed deep into his heart. Madeline could see the life was sucked out of him as he fell to the floor. The snake disintegrated and vanished.

CHAPTER 39

Ciaran drowned in darkness and oblivion. His mind was the only part of him that was alert. His body was numb, and his physical strength no longer existed. His energy had been reduced to zero. At that moment, he understood Iilos more than ever—more precisely, her feeling of having her entire existence reduced to a mind.

People typically referred to having a strong mind as being important, but by itself, it was worthless. Iilos had tried for hundreds of years to keep her mind active, and she had made a difference by helping people. What could he do if his mind was the only thing he had left?

At this moment, he was certain his physical existence was dying. This was his battle. There was nothing more Madeline could do for him.

Dan had alerted him about the cobra, and he had ignored the warning. The legendary cobra had bitten Re, the first pharaoh, and had taken his power. Ciaran didn't care about the power. At the moment, his only desire was to come back to his wife and the children he was about to see.

He couldn't bear the thought of watching his children from a distance. But wanting wasn't enough, he had to take action. He had Lyla—she was his last resource. She would help him. He was reluctant when he spoke the spell, but he did make that exchange with her.

He heard Iilos's voice. "Make him call Lyla."

Then he heard Madeline respond, "Didn't he do that before with Hoyt? Can he say it twice?"

"He said nothing before. He only pretended to make Hoyt say the other spell."

Ciaran wanted to smile, but he couldn't move. He knew what he had to do, but he couldn't physically do it now. He tried again. Nothing worked. He couldn't open his eyes to see anything or his mouth to say anything.

He knew he was dying, and if he didn't say the spell, there was nothing Lyla could do.

He kept drowning in the dark, bottomless hole.

Then, in front of him, the image of Lyla appeared, floating above him in the dark water. She had slid into his subconsciousness. She smiled at him and reached out her hand to him.

"Say the spell. Free me into your world, Ciaran," she said.

In his mind, he said, "Antallagí."

Lyla's image glowed like a rainbow. She smiled at him, kissed his forehead, and said, "Thank you."

"The gratitude is mine, Lyla," he said.

"Do you believe in my fairy tales now, Ciaran?"

"Yes, I do. I believe in miracles now. There are many things science cannot explain. But miracles can only come from selfless individuals, saints, and people like you, Lyla. I owe you my life. Whatever I do, whoever I save, it's your doing."

Lyla smiled. Her body glowed, and she disintegrated into nothingness.

His strength had come back to him. Ciaran pushed himself back up through the surface of consciousness.

He opened his eyes and found wedges of light coming from the dome ceilings. Madeline touched his face. "There you are. Welcome back."

The light from the dome ceiling was extremely bright, suggesting the coronation elements had been in place and ready. Madeline helped him up and walked with him to the glass chamber. Before she left, he grabbed her hand and kissed it. "Thank you," he said.

"You don't have to thank me for threatening to cut your head off. After all, we're married."

He grinned as she walked away from the closing door.

***

Ciaran pressed his palm on the control panel. His key stone glowed and spun in fiery red.

Energy sparked and shot out of the chamber and out of the room, exploding into the sky.

He could see the Sciphil screens outside. Tadgh and Jo had made it to their control panels. The energy from all active Sciphils was connected to the king tower. They all looked at him with pride.

An ocean of energy flowed into him. His energy and his body were reborn. He was now carrying the energy source of the king of one of the most powerful universes. And two things remained intact—his mind and his love.

After a while, the process completed, he exited the glass chamber and approached Madeline. They turned together toward the public screens.

The Eudaizian air vibrated with joy as people celebrated a new era of life. The citizens turned and looked straight into the screens with anticipation. Then the public went silent, and the quietness was contagious from district to district.

"What are they waiting for?" Madeline asked.

Ciaran nodded toward the public screens with understanding. He turned around, pulled Madeline into his arms, and kissed her. The joy exploded across all of Eudaiz.

When they finished with the kiss, he turned on a private channel. "Jake, can you handle the publicity?"

Jake came on the screen instantly. "Yes, sir. If you could just hold the kiss a little longer so that I can take a snapshot for the poster. It's good for publicity."

"Jake!" Ciaran growled.

"Okay, sure, Ciaran. I can use some old images. I'll put something on the public screens now so you can go."

"Thank you."

Ciaran held Madeline's hand as they left the control panel. They exited the tower with Iilos beside them.

Outside the tower, thousands of soldiers cheered. Gaia left the commander and darted toward Ciaran and Madeline. When she saw Iilos, she stopped.

"Mother?" she asked, her voice shaky as she waited for confirmation from Iilos.

Ciaran knew Iilos couldn't possibly be Gaia's mother. If she denied it, he would take Gaia in and care for her. He squeezed Madeline's hand slightly. She squeezed back—a gesture of agreement.

Iilos crouched in front of Gaia, "Yes, Gaia, I am your mother. Don't you like how I look?"

Gaia cried, "Yes, Mother. You're beautiful."

Iilos held Gaia in her arms. Together, they stood and turned to walk away. Gaia turned back to give Ciaran and Madeline a wave goodbye.

"Where are you taking her?" Ciaran asked.

"Iilos, the home Mother has found for me," Iilos said. "It has my name on it." She smiled and walked away with Gaia.

CHAPTER 40

Ciaran and Madeline entered their bedchamber in Sciphil Three residence. It was still early, and they had no intention of going to bed. They intended to get changed and then go to the Daimon Gate to visit the children. The adrenaline of the day was still running strong in their veins.

Ciaran could see the emotion on Madeline's face, and he did what he had longed for most during their hard day—he pulled her into his arms and kissed her.

He had been starving for her all day. It was his coronation day—a significant day not only for him but for all citizens in this universe. But through all the danger and activities of the day, he had focused on her—his wife, the mother of his children, the love of his life.

Only with her could he survive anything.

That was his secret. It wasn't the king energy. It wasn't the muscles or the brain power. As long as he knew his family was safe, he was ready to face any challenges.

He and Madeline embraced and clung to each other for a long moment, blocking the universe out of their world, until a holocast beamed in. At the other end of the beam stood Jennifer and Conan, the twins in their arms.

Ciaran held Madeline's shoulders tightly as they shook from emotion. Tears rolled down Madeline's face as she saw their children who had now joined their world. They had a family. When the emotion started shaking Ciaran's body, he squeezed Madeline's shoulders tighter.

The children were beautiful. They looked at Madeline and him with their large, dark gray eyes. They smiled—no, that had to be his imagination. Children this young wouldn't see much regardless of how special they were. There were no miracles when it came to child development.

But his children's mere existence was a miracle to him. Lyla was right all those years ago. He should believe in miracles.

It was the first time in his life that he was short of words. Everything in his mind was jumbled together, and he was afraid that if he spoke, it wouldn't be coherent.

Seeing their reaction, Jennifer said, "Well, the girl complains she doesn't have a name yet."

"Lyla," Madeline said and looked up at Ciaran. "Is that okay with you?" she asked.

"Yes." He was glad he could find an answer. He cleared his throat. "Yes, Lyla is a good name."

"Oh, and the boy said he doesn't want to be called Caedmon," Conan said.

"That's nonnegotiable because he's named after a Titan. And his mother made that promise." Ciaran grinned. "Thank you both for taking care of the children. I know it's been difficult."

Conan shrugged. "It's nothing. Just practice for Tadgh and Jo's baby."

"What?" Madeline asked.

"You should really be careful about saying *baby*, Conan. It might be babies!" Jennifer said.

"What?" Ciaran asked.

"Why are you so surprised? Tadgh said you arranged the ring for him," Conan said.

Ciaran replied, "Yes, but he didn't mention anything about Jo being pregnant when I sent them on a mission this morning."

"My little friend, with her vicious, foxy determination, would never let Tadgh turn down a mission on your coronation day because of her." Madeline grinned. "But I'll have a word with her about not letting me be the first to know."

"Now in that, you're mistaken," Ciaran said. "Husband trumps best friend. Big time."

She punched his chest. "Are you sure about that?"

"Punch away. It's a multiversal truth." Ciaran laughed.

"Will you be here for Christmas?" Jennifer asked.

"There is no Christmas in Eudaiz," Ciaran said.

"There is in the Daimon Gate. And by the way, you're king now. Why don't you create a Christmas in Eudaiz?" Jennifer said.

"Nice thought," Madeline agreed.

Ciaran smiled. "I'll think about it, Mother."

Jennifer smiled and, in front of an astonished Ciaran and Madeline, she said, "All right. Take your time. But we'll hang on to your children until you come here for Christmas. Now it's time for them to go to bed." Then she cooed, "You're sleepy, aren't you little ones?" Conan smiled and switched the holocast off.

Ciaran turned toward Madeline and lifted her chin up. "Would you like to create a Christmas in Eudaiz, my First Councillor?" he asked.

"Yes, but I wouldn't call it Christmas."

Ciaran smiled. "The LeBlancs built the constitution for the entire Eudaizian universe. Instituting a Christmas-like event couldn't be that difficult. Christmas trees are fine. But no Santa Claus allowed."

"Why not?"

"Well, Eudaizians are too rigid to play Santa Claus. Getting one from Earth would mean I'd have to give him a permit and then train him. The Xiiloks are okay if we talk to the right people, but a Santa Claus with wormy irises can't be all too child-friendly."

Madeline laughed. Ciaran spun her around and muffled her laughter with a passionate kiss.

THE END

BONUS SHORT STORY >>> NEXT

BONUS
SHORT STORY

THE STOLEN

The muffled scream of a child cut through the darkness.

His silhouette shook as he tried to wriggle free of the hands wrapped around his neck belonging to a large man looming over him.

One twist of the hands and the fragile bone of the child's neck would be savaged.

In a single second, everything would end for the boy.

Flash.

His fury had wings. It moved as fast as light and it killed without mercy, without discrimination.

All he had to do was free it.

Today was the day he was born thirty years ago. Tonight was the night he had to kill a man to save a child.

All he had to do was to free it; his Daimon.

His father was philosophical about the Daimon. It was a spirit that was supposed to keep one righteous. But his was violent. There was nothing philosophical about violence, righteous or not.

A kill was a kill.

It was beyond reason. At least that was his father's ideology.

Thing was, his father was no longer with him. Even if his father looked down from Heaven, if there was such a place, and didn't approve of his action; there was nothing his father could do about it. More importantly, he was not to live for anyone's approval. He was his own self and he was the most independent child his father had ever trained.

Independence was the first lesson his father gave him. Since he was two, his father had home-schooled and trained him to make the most of his potential. At five, his physics and his intellect excelled. And at the same time, his father discovered that his talent came with a package: violence.

The talent and the violence made the whole of him. Together, they formed his Daimon.

To his father's expectations, he had learned to utilize his intellect and had suppressed his fury. But he had never promised not to try his fury, to see what it offered. His father had said, too many times, that he was a normal human being. Well, if he was to believe that, he could just be a normal child for once; naughty and curious.

And he saw what his fury did.

When he sent out a flash of his fury, he chopped down ten old trees to the root in one swift hit. The trees Father had been talking about calling in bulldozers to clear the path to the hill, but never found time to do so.

The morning his father told him that a weird storm during the night had conveniently cleared the little bush in their backyard, he'd said nothing. What could a four year old child do with such 'catastrophe'?

He never let his fury out since then. For the most part, when he feared it was getting out of control, he took it out physically on inanimate objects. His furniture hated him.

He got better over the years and learned more of how to control it to a certain extent. One thing had become clear, his fury was not psychological nor was it philosophical; it was primal. It was a beast and it lived in his blood.

He inched closer into the tunnel and the silhouettes had become more prominent, printing against the background of a fast-moving train. The noise of the train covered the scream of the child, and was why only his mind heard the child, and no one else. One second and it would be all over. He could send out his fury right now and save the child.

But, his fury would decapitate the man in front of the child.

Which was worse, dead or witness a decapitation and have blood and gore rain on him? He couldn't speak for the child.

He took over his father's corporate world when he was a teenager; and he was a predator in the business. His intellect was his lethal weapon; and he had not run into any opponents he couldn't defeat. At the same time, although he hadn't spent a day on the street struggling to make a living, nothing about human behavior surprised him. That was his basic training.

Artificial intelligence, computer science, biology, psychology, chemistry, astrology and the like. They were his toys when he was a kid.

His father swore to him that he was normal!

But now, in front of him was an extraordinary situation of two ordinary human beings. Beneath the obvious size differences of the people in conflict, the silhouettes gave him no additional information. Who was in danger here? The child? The man? Or himself? What if this was a trap to lure him into the tunnel?

He thought he found his soul mate. She understood him and his Daimon. She understood him and his ambition to change life and the landscape of science. She understood his pain. She thrived to make him happy and it had cost her life. She died making him a present for this thirtieth birthday.

Today.

Before he ran himself to the ground with guilt, he found evidence for all the objections to their marriage. He wouldn't label it the way people did, betrayal. It couldn't be a betrayal if she didn't promise him her loyalty first. They loved each other, of that, he was sure. He was even surer that he loved her.

He had run on empty for a few weeks as the world blurred by. He had a responsibility. He had people who depended on him. He had to keep going.

Today, the meeting in freezing winter in New York was a good break from his London office – a place full of painful memories. But as soon as the meeting finished, he circled back to his empty self. He didn't know where his Daimon was, but he was sure a large part of his soul was missing.

His assistant all but begged him not to go for a walk in the snow.

And here he was, standing in front of a tunnel. At the other end were the silhouettes of two people, one of whom he should kill to save the other.

All he had to do was to let his Daimon free.

One second. That was enough time to send out his fury and kill the man. It wasn't the killing decision he was hesitant about; it was who actually needed his help. He stepped further into the tunnel and yelled, "Stop!"

It wasn't the authority or the meaning of the word that stopped the man. It was the intention behind it. The intention to follow suit if the command was not obeyed. The intention to cause harm if necessary.

The man dropped the kid down to his feet.

He had walked halfway through the dark tunnel. Dim light flickered from the other end. He recalled the horror in his assistant's eyes when he said he wanted to go for a walk by himself at this hour in an unsavory part of New York.

"Who the fuck do you think you are?" the man grunted out the words.

He was only a few feet away. It wasn't the man he wanted to see, he needed to see the child. He needed to look into the child's eyes and be certain he had made the right decision.

"This ain't your fucking business. Hear me?"

He kept walking toward the child and the man. The child let out a little moan as the man lifted him up a few inches from the ground, still holding the collar of his shirt. The moan earned the child a slap in the head.

"Stop! Don't make me hurt you," he warned.

He was close enough and he could see the child's eyes now; frightened.

The man kept hitting the boy. "He's mine. I can do whatever I want to him."

There was no need to send his fury out now. He was close enough to break the man's neck with his hands.

"Let the kid go," he said.

"You're a fucking idiot. He had to earn his keep. I can't feed him forever." The man grabbed the kid and dragged him away.

"Leave the kid," he said.

The man stopped, turned around, dropped the child, mumbled some profanity and charged at him. In the dim light, he saw the reflection of a knife. He sidestepped the approach. In one swift move, the man landed on his back, still gripping the knife. The man jumped up to his feet and lunged at him again.

The man didn't give him a choice.

Years of combat training weren't wasted on him. He actually liked it for the most part. The power of body and mind control and what the human body could achieve with the appropriate manipulation of movement always fascinated him. He blocked the second attack, and before the man could thrust the knife at him for the third time, the man's knife had pierced his own throat.

Blood spurted, splattered on him and the child. The man slumped to the ground.

Dead.

He turned and looked at the child. The big brown eyes filled with tears, his small shoulders shook with fear as he stared down at the body of the man on the ground. But he didn't run.

"What's your name?"

The child blinked. "Little Mike."

"That's not your real name."

"Michael Fraser."

He smiled. "That's a lot better. Who's this man, Michael?"

"My stepfather." Michael frowned and played with the hem of his jumper.

"Why did he try to hurt you?"

"He didn't try. He just hurt me." Michael was still examining the hem of his jumper.

He lifted Michael's chin up and looked into his eyes. "Where are your parents?"

"I've never met my father. Mom died last year."

"How old are you?"

"Eight. I don't go to school, if that's your next question." Michael stared straight up at him and didn't go back to the hem of his jumper.

"Do you understand what I just did to your stepfather and why?"

Michael nodded. "He hurt me. You told him to stop but he didn't. He tried to do you with the knife, but he copped that knife in the end. He deserves it."

A cold breeze blasted his face. It wasn't the chill of New York's winter, but the tenacious tone and meaning of what Michael had said that stunned him.

He now understood how his father felt when he made his first explosive compound and blew off the head of the Goddess of Kindness statue in their backyard. His father knew about the fury, the violence; but it was the first time reality dawned on his father that, regardless of how much his son could control himself, the violence would take the better part of him.

His father was devastated; he knew it now, twenty five years later.

He looked at Michael. "Nobody deserves to die, and no one has the right to murder."

"If you didn't kill him, he'd have killed you. Then he'd have killed me. Who would say he doesn't have the right to murder if we had both died?"

"Michael, I killed him in self-defense. That's a totally different matter. But I provoked him first. I did that because I know I can protect myself. What did you do to provoke him, knowing you can't protect yourself?"

"I told him I'd kill him sooner or later."

When he saw the grimace filling Michael's face, a chill crept into his blood. He mentally took a step back from the child. "How did you plan to do that?"

"I ain't have no planning. That was before. But I know now. If I have to kill someone, it will be in self-defense."

He crouched so his eyes were level with Michael's. "Self-defense is not a trick to get away with murder. I don't want to be the one to put that idea into your head. Perhaps, you're too young to understand, but I need to ..."

"I'm not too young. I'm eight years old. I know the most important thing a man gotta do, is to keep his promises. I keep my promises. If he didn't know how to keep his promises, he didn't deserve to live," Michael raised his voice and pointed at the dead man's body.

"Yes, Michael. Keeping promises is very important. But it's not how you judge whether a person deserves to live. In fact, you don't have the right to judge whether anyone deserves to live or die."

"So who will have a say for Nick? He got killed and he has no say. It's unfair. Nick just wanted to protect me. Just like what you did. You can defend yourself, but Nick can't. Nick wanted him to get his hands off of me and ... he killed Nick for that ...he promised my mom he'd care for us... he never did... all he did was hurt me ..." Michael's lips trembled, his shoulders shook with the chill and the emotions, tears filled his eyes but he refused to let them fall.

"Who's Nick?"

"My friend. My only friend. He's the one who made the money, keep the food coming in. But he's still not happy. He wanted more!" Michael pointed at his stepfather.

He could feel his blood boiling. "He killed a kid for not making him enough money?"

Tears started falling down Michael's face. "He shouldn't have bitten him ... I can take a few slaps and punches. I can take it, I told Nick that, but he wouldn't listen. He kept biting and barking until he turned around and broke his neck ..."

"Barking? Is Nick a dog?"

Michael hitched up, almost choking with his tears. "... Yes... his mom died, so my mom brought him home when I was little. He grew up fast and when I didn't have enough warm clothes last winter, he lied on top of me like a blanket."

He reached out a hand to wipe the tears on Michael's face, but the child backed up.

"He made Nick do all the tricks on the road to distract people so I can pick pockets ... days after days, nights after nights ... we were freezing, no food, no warm clothes, but we brought home the money. I promised Nick when we save enough money, I'll run and I'll take him with me. But we don't have enough yet..."

Michael shivered. His jumper was obviously not enough to keep the chill off him. He reached out to Michael, but the child once more backed out. Tears still streamed down Michael's face regardless how many times he wiped.

"We tried. But it's winter. People won't get out that much. We couldn't get much money. He cut off our food and hit me. That was when Nick got angry. I told him not to... I can take it ... but he kept biting until ... until he grabbed his neck and twisted it broken. ... Nick can't defend himself ... he provoked that man to get himself killed ..." Michael gasped for air.

"He had no right to hit you. For that he would go to jail. But you can't say you'd kill him because of what he did to Nick. I understand you're upset and Nick is your friend ..."

"Is this because Nick is a dog?"

He simply didn't know how to respond without digging deeper into the wound.

"I promised Nick I'm going to get him out of here. I couldn't keep my promise. Without Nick, I can't pick any pockets. Then he beat me more... and more ... just now ... I told him I'm going to kill him. He got angry. He's going to do what he did to Nick. He's going to break my neck tonight. But I'm ready for it... I want to see my mom ..."

Michael swayed, on the verge of passing out. He pulled at the kid and wrapped his arms around him. "When was the last time you ate something?"

"Can't remember ..."

He took off his thick coat and wrapped it around Michael. The coat was too big for the boy to walk in so he carried him in his arms. Michael's head lulled against the crook of his neck and stayed there for a short moment.

He walked along the tunnel to the main road. When he nearly got to the road, Michael stirred and straightened his head. "Where are we going?"

"Hospital. I need to put some food into you, but we have blood all over us. If we go to a food stall, they'll call the cops. So, the hospital seems to be appropriate. I want the doctor to check you out, too."

"No, go to the cops. The police station is just around the corner. We have a dead body in the tunnel and he ain't a dog."

"I can take care of that after I take you to the hospital. I'll call for a car now."

"You mean a cab?"

"No, my company car," he responded, and then remembered he had left his cell phone in the boardroom after the meeting. He must have caused his assistant a panic attack by now. "Damn it!" he cursed.

Michael laughed out loud.

"What's funny?"

"You talk pretty, so I didn't think you'd swear."

"You mean my British accent."

"No. That makes you sound funny. But your words are pretty. I like them. Mom has pretty words, too. She'd been to school for many, many years. She said she wanted me to go to school, too. She never got around to do it. We moved around a lot. Then she ran into him…"

"Did he get violent with your mother?"

Michael said nothing and leaned into the crook of his neck again. "Okay. I won't ask. Now, I don't have my phone with me, so I have to walk to the main road to hail a taxi …"

"Police station, just around the corner," Michael mumbled.

He kept walking.

"Cabs won't go this way. You can only get them at the rank."

"Would you mind telling me where the rank is? Or I'll go to the main road and ask someone."

"They have food at the police station."

He kept walking.

"You're shaking."

"Yes, I'm cold because you're wearing my coat."

"Okay, you'll find cabs on the left, turn there and cross that little street."

He followed Michael's instructions and ended up at the police station. He pushed the door in. A blast of warm air inside greeted them with the bonus of a dozen pairs of eyes staring at the blood on their clothes.

"Put me down, I look like a scarecrow," Michael said. He put Michael down on the floor and the coat pooled on the floor. Michael took the coat off and gave it back to him.

Seeing the blood, the officer at the front counter gave them immediate attention and got them into an interviewing room, separate from the main foyer.

"Officer, we have an incident to report, but the kid hasn't eaten for days. Could you get him something?"

One officer went for the food and another remained in the interviewing room. The first officer soon returned with a sandwich and a bottle of water.

Before he could say anything, and before the officer took a seat with his notepad, Michael said, "I found him like that in the tunnel. Dead. Blood everywhere. He said he'd get some dinner, but I waited for a long time. So I went out and looked for him. I found him in the tunnel." Then Michael pointed at him, "Then Mr. Pretty Talk found me and took me here. I was scared shitless." Michael bit into the sandwich.

He arched an eyebrow and opened his mouth to say something, but Michael cut in again. "I can sort things out with the officer here. So, you can go now."

"I beg your pardon?" he said.

"The kid said he's fine and you can go. I know the guy Michael's talking about. He's a regular here," the officer said.

"Who's the regular? Michael or his stepfather?"

"Both. His stepfather, if he deserves the title, is the worst kind of junkie. Someone is going to do him in one day. Let's hope today is the day." The officer shook his head and made notes on his writing pad.

"But I found them, shouldn't I give a statement?"

"Ciaran LeBlanc, is it? Sorry if I didn't say your name right." Michael put Ciaran's wallet on the table. "Old habits die hard."

Ciaran smiled. "Now that's pretty talk."

"Mom taught me," Michael grinned. "Didn't mean to pick your wallet. I just wanted to know your name."

"You could have asked me."

Michael took another bite of the sandwich and spoke with a mouth full, "Man, if ya told me, I wouldn't get the spelling right."

"It's shouldn't be a problem if you go to school."

Michael arched an eyebrow. "School doesn't feed me."

"You're saying if you didn't have to worry about food, you would go to school?"

Michael contemplated, but said nothing in response.

"Can you promise me if you don't have to worry about food, you will go to school? I know you're a man of his word."

Michael kept chowing down on the sandwich and shook his head. "I can do this myself. Don't need ya no more." Michael gave Ciaran a dismissive shrug.

Ciaran nodded. "All right then."

He stood up and signaled the officer to take him out. When Ciaran was at the door of the interviewing room, Michael said, "I want more."

Ciaran turned around and arched an eyebrow. "And what else would you like?"

The officer chuckled.

"I go to school, I'll need pocket money. I need to buy clothes, books and all sort of ..."

"All right, you will have an allowance. What else?"

Michael stood up and approached Ciaran. "I will give you your money back and I want it on paper. I want a man to write it down on paper."

Ciaran frowned. "You want me to give you an allowance and have my lawyer put it in writing?"

The officer's jaw dropped and he glared at Michael.

"No. I want your lawyer to write down that I owe you the money and I will pay you back when I grow up. I want to have that paper."

Ciaran nodded. "I'll send my lawyer tomorrow to draw up the paperwork." He glanced at the door of the police station and saw his company car had arrived. Ciaran nodded toward the officer at the counter, thanking him for making the arrangement. Then he turned back to Michael. "I have to go now."

Michael nodded.

"If you want to keep in touch, all you have to do is to ask me. You don't have to hang onto a piece of paper."

"Are you going home now?"

Ciaran nodded. "Yes. I am flying to London tonight."

"When will you be back here?"

"I am not sure. I'll have to check my schedule."

Michael smiled. "See! I need that paper."

Ciaran laughed. "You're a very smart boy. You'll do well at school. Learn everything you can, make a lot of money and pay me back your loan."

"I promise." Michael said solemnly, his eyes gleamed with tears. Ciaran opened his arms. Michael dove in and hugged him.

Ciaran left for the car. Before Ciaran got in, he heard Michael call out. He turned and saw Michael standing at the door of the police station with his palm open, revealing a pocket watch. Michael approached. Ciaran crouched to avoid having his six foot three height towering over Michael.

"I'm sorry. I just wanted a souvenir. Couldn't take this one. It's your father's watch." He gave it back to Ciaran.

Ciaran took the watch, rubbing his thumb on the engraved text, "The love of my life - Conan LeBlanc." He smiled. "I actually stole this from my father."

Michael eyes widened. "You steal?"

Ciaran nodded and winked at Michael.

"Did your father find out?"

Ciaran shook his head.

"You're so cool!"

Ciaran laughed.

"Will you visit me when you come back to New York?"

"Of course, I promise. You can keep this watch if you like, as proof I will be coming back for it."

Michael shook his head. "I have your word and the paper. That's enough. You need that watch more than me."

"What do you mean?"

"In the tunnel, when I said I was ready for him to break my neck, I meant it. Nick was the only thing I had left from my mom and he took Nick from me. When you walked into the tunnel, I saw the light. Mom always said the light would come for me one day, and everything would get better. You brought me the light. I haven't said thank you for that."

"You're welcome." Ciaran smiled and slid the watch back into his pocket.

"Don't let anyone take the watch from you."

"I won't, I promise. Now get back inside, you're shivering."

Michael rushed in and hugged Ciaran tightly one last time, turned on his heel, and then scurried inside the building.

Ciaran stepped into the world of his familiars; inside his long black limousine. As the car left the police station behind, Ciaran saw Michael peeking from inside the door of the police station. He rubbed his thumb on his pocket watch. His mother had given the watch to his father when they were dating.

If he hadn't stolen the pocket watch off his father, he wouldn't have any personal item from him. The business empire and legacy his father left behind wasn't for him, but for the family. Everything his father had done was to make him a better man and to make the most out of his potential.

But he occasionally wanted to be just a kid, though he knew he was raised for an important cause, whatever it was. He would deal with it when it came his way.

But for now, he was glad Michael had returned the watch. He'd stolen it from his father, and he was still proud of it. He was glad he walked into the tunnel tonight.

He saved the life of a child and, at the same time, had saved a part of his soul.

For all of that, he's grateful.

The End

For a limited time, D.N. Leo gives away
4 books in the Multiverse Collection

CLAIM YOUR FREE E-BOOKS
http://narrativeland.com

THANK YOU FOR READING!
D.N. LEO

D.N. LEO 'S NOVELS
SERIES READING ORDER

http://narrativeland.com/dnleonovels

—

A SHADE OF MIND
(narrativeland.com/shade)
Main Characters: Ciaran, Madeline, Tadgh, and Jo
(Recommended reading in order)
1-4 Random Psychic
2-4 Forever Mortal
3-4 Elusive Beings
4-4 Imperfect Divine

—

SPECTRUM
(narrativeland.com/spectrum)
Main characters: Lorcan, Orla, Roy and Mori
(Recommended reading in order)
1-4 White Curse
2-4 Blue Fox
3-4 Indigo Stone
4-4 Red Moon

—

MINDSCAPE
(narrativeland.com/mind)
Main characters:
Ciaran, Madeline, Tadgh, Jo, Kyle, Hoyt, Ayana, Pete,
Sizx, Lorcan, Orla
(Recommended reading in order within series, can be
read in ANY order in related to other series)

Queen's Gambit
Knight & Pawn
Lone Castle
Doubled Bishops
Dead Squares
King's Endgame

—

SILVER BLOOD
Main characters:
(narrativeland.com/silver)
Ciaran, Madeline, Tadgh, Jo, Caedmon, Sedna, Roy,
Mori, Zach, Mya, Lorcan and Orla
This series can be read in ANY order within the series
and in related to other series.

Virgo
Libra
Scorpio
Taurus
Pisces
Gemini

Thank you for reading.

If you enjoyed reading **Mindscape Three**, I would appreciate it if you would help others enjoy this book, too.

Recommend it. Please help other readers find this book by recommending it to friends, readers' groups and discussion boards.

Review it. Please tell other readers why you liked this book by reviewing it wherever you purchase the book from. If you do write a review, please send me an email at info@dnleo.com so I can thank you with a personal email.

COPYRIGHT

MINDSCAPE THREE

By D.N. Leo

I greatly appreciate you taking the time to read my work. Please consider leaving a review wherever you purchased the book, and refer the book to your friends.